THE MAKING OF

STAR TREK® II
THE WRATH OF KHAN

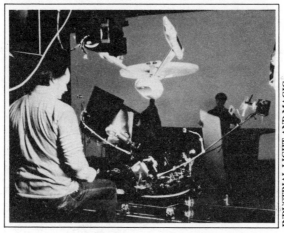

**The behind-the-scenes story
of *Star Trek*'s greatest adventure!**

Paramount Pictures Presents
STAR TREK® II
THE WRATH OF KHAN
Starring
WILLIAM SHATNER   LEONARD NIMOY
DeFOREST KELLEY
Co-Starring
JAMES DOOHAN   WALTER KOENIG
GEORGE TAKEI   NICHELLE NICHOLS
Also Starring
BIBI BESCH
and
PAUL WINFIELD as Terrell
Introducing KIRSTIE ALLEY as Saavik
and Starring RICARDO MONTALBAN as Khan
Music Composed by JAMES HORNER
Executive Consultant GENE RODDENBERRY
Based on STAR TREK
created by GENE RODDENBERRY
Executive Producer HARVE BENNETT
Screenplay by JACK B. SOWARDS
Story by HARVE BENNETT
and JACK B. SOWARDS
Produced by ROBERT SALLIN
Directed by NICHOLAS MEYER
A Paramount Picture

THE WRATH OF KHAN

THE MAKING OF

STAR TREK® II

THE WRATH OF KHAN

ALLAN ASHERMAN

PUBLISHED BY POCKET BOOKS NEW YORK

Most Pocket Books are available at special quantity discounts for bulk purchases for sales promotions, premiums or fund raising. Special books or book excerpts can also be created to fit specific needs.

For details write or telephone the office of the Vice President of Special Markets, Pocket Books, 1230 Avenue of the Americas, New York, New York 10020. (212) 245-6400, ext. 1760.

Another *Original* publication of POCKET BOOKS

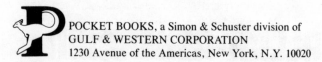

POCKET BOOKS, a Simon & Schuster division of
GULF & WESTERN CORPORATION
1230 Avenue of the Americas, New York, N.Y. 10020

ISBN: 0-671-46182-6

First Pocket Books printing October, 1982

10 9 8 7 6 5 4 3 2 1

Printed in the U.S.A.

Dedication

Dedicated to Mr. Harve Bennett, the Executive Producer and coordinating, driving force behind *Star Trek II: The Wrath of Khan,* for conscientiously and successfully perpetuating the STAR TREK dream.

With special appreciation to Mr. Gene Roddenberry, the creator of STAR TREK, from whose fertile imagination sprang this entire phenomenon.

And to all the individuals who made it possible for me to complete this book within my extremely tight deadline.

Acknowledgments

Paramount—Edward Egan, Dianne Mandell, Pat Perry, Tom Phillips, Susan Pyle

Deborah Arakelian, Harve Bennett, Merritt Blake, James Horner, Joseph R. Jennings, DeForest Kelley, Ronnie Leaf, Nicholas Meyer, Leonard Nimoy, Sylvia Rubinstein, Robert Sallin, Teresa Victor

ILM—Terry Chostner, Rose Duignan

Pocket Books—John Douglas, David Hartwell, Mimi Panitch

Agents—Lea Braff, Sharon Jarvis

Special thanks to Mr. Craig Miller for the use of his office, without which this manuscript could not have been produced

Dedicated to all the fans of STAR TREK, and to Mr. Harve Bennett for perpetuating the dream

Contents

Introduction

On a summer day in 1966, I boarded a bus and traveled, adventuring alone, to Cleveland, Ohio, and my first World Science Fiction Convention. That trip led me to explore farther beyond the borders of my home territory, Brooklyn, New York, than I could ever have suspected. That bus trip introduced me to the wonders of appreciating science fiction's voyages of imagination with others who relished these mental excursions.

At that convention, I was also privileged to see both pilot films of *Star Trek* before the series' television debut. That weekend I met Gene Roddenberry's wonderful concept of futuristic exploration, harmony and hope. I made new friends who lived in a neighborhood far removed from my own.

Subsequently, I would become involved in the successful letter-writing campaigns to save *Star Trek* from being cancelled. I would grieve when it *was* cancelled and, like so many of the real-life friends I met as a result of my *Star Trek* fan-related activities, I would decide that this constructive perception of humanity's future would never become a thing of the past.

Together with others in the New York area, I would become involved in the plans to hold the very first *Star Trek* conventions in that area; as one of "The Committee" I would contribute to letting the characters and concepts of *Star Trek* survive in the minds of their devotees.

There were frustrations then, too. The first rumor of a *Star Trek* motion picture, or a new series of television episodes, surfaced as early as 1972, but none of these reported productions ever reached completion until Paramount Pictures released *Star Trek: The Motion Picture* in 1979. It was thrilling when the dream of *Star Trek* came visually alive again, with millions of dollars spent to recreate the starship *U.S.S. Enterprise,* her crew and her missions of exploration.

Then came the first rumors that Paramount Pictures had given the go-ahead for production of a new *Star Trek* adventure. There were, at first, some doubts about whether this would be a theatrical motion picture or a made-for-television movie. There were also other mutterings throughout *Star Trek* fandom, but none of these things mattered. What *did* matter was that the *Star Trek* format was recognized as being commercially successful, and that we *would* be seeing another *Trek* production, with possibly more to come.

With the release of the motion picture *Star Trek II: The Wrath of Khan,* it became clear that the film is successful both as a business entity and as a direct, accurate expansion on the earlier *Trek* productions.

Star Trek II: The Wrath of Khan is an excellent motion picture no matter how you look at it. It takes itself seriously, but not *too* seriously. It has fun with the *Trek* characters, but not *too* much fun. Most important, it continues the series' initial aim of space explorations that people can learn from.

The success of *Star Trek II,* like the success of any well-executed work of art, is no accident. It is due to the many people associated wtih the production, cast and crew alike. Their dedicated labors allowed them to create the characters, events and locales that brought the film so wonderfully to life. It was a complex and laborious process. Such is the magic of motion pictures, however, that we, the audience, perceive one finished, symmetrical and successful product.

Just as the motion picture itself has a story to tell, the individuals and events that led to the completion of *Star Trek II: The Wrath of Khan* are stories unto themselves. The evolution of the film, the expectations of *Trek* fans all over the world and the well-deserved success of this motion picture is the story of *The Making of Star Trek II.*

THE MAKING OF

STAR TREK® II

THE WRATH OF KHAN

Executive producer Harve Bennett and the crew of the U.S.S. *Enterprise* on the bridge for *Star Trek II: The Wrath of Khan*

Early Speculations

As the box office figures for *Star Trek: The Motion Picture* started to mount up, it became increasingly apparent that there would probably be another *Star Trek* movie produced. For a few months after the first feature film was issued, the question was whether or not others would be made at all. Following that period, however, the question then became when the film would be made, whether it would be a theatrical or a television movie, and what it would be about.

At first, as with any project concerning *Star Trek,* the rumors ran rampant. Everybody and his brother had been signed to appear in the film, which would feature everyone who had ever appeared in the *Star Trek* television series. The movie would be about eight hours long. It would be seen on television in the form of a miniseries.

While all these stories circulated, however, the majority of *Star Trek* fans realized that anything they heard about the movie at that early date would almost surely be nothing but rumors.

A report in *Newsday,* a Long Island (New York City suburban) newspaper, confirmed that both William Shatner and Leonard Nimoy had been signed up to do the movie, which would (it was announced) be out "next summer."

The next day, *Newsday* reported that Nicholas Meyer had been signed to direct the film. After a listing of Meyer's credits, the article proceeded to confuse the issue of *Star Trek II*'s ultimate distribution. The film, said the piece, was to be produced by Paramount's television division, and it would likely be released theatrically as a *test,* remaining a theatrical release if successful or winding up on Cable TV instead.

The article further mentioned the budget of *Star Trek II* as "less than $10 million."

The final sentence of the piece started a whole new wave of speculations and rumors. It was a simple declaration that one of the villains featured in the television series would be "resurrected" for the film.

Immediately *Star Trek* fans began comparing notes about who would be the returning baddie. Initial guessers thought that a Klingon would be a good bet for a return bout. Perhaps it would be Kor, the first Klingon of the series, who was originally supposed to return in the episode "The Trouble With Tribbles." If not Kor, then perhaps Captain Koloth, the character who replaced Kor in "Tribbles." Maybe *another* Klingon would be back, another actor portraying a Klingon from the series. There was some speculation that Mark Lenard, the actor who had portrayed a Romulan, then the father of Spock in *Trek* TV episodes and the Klingon commander in *Star Trek: The Motion Picture,* would be the new villain.

Perhaps it wouldn't be a Klingon at all, reasoned some fans. A Romulan, a renegade Organian, a berserk Vulcan, a vengeful Tellerite or Andorian . . . any of these would be excellent antagonists for Kirk.

There were other speculations just as intriguing. Perhaps Gary Mitchell, Kirk's old friend who had been transformed into a super-menace in "Where No Man Has Gone Before," was not really dead. Or . . . the newspaper piece *did* use the word *resurrected.* Perhaps they meant it literally! This supposition opened still more doors of possible choices. Maybe the Romulan commander of "Balance of Terror" (one of Mark Lenard's roles) would be brought back. Perhaps it would be Kodos, the Executioner (otherwise known as actor Anton Karidian in "The Conscience of the King"), who was to return.

Undoubtedly, fans thought of other possibilities, including Charles Evans (the super-powered adolescent of "Charlie X"), the incorrigible Harry Mudd, or the female Romulan commander seen in "The Enterprise Incident." All these individuals definitely had grudges against Captain (or Admiral) Kirk.

Or maybe, just *maybe*, Kirk would be pitted against *himself*, in a repetition of the transporter malfunction that divided the Captain into two halves in "The Enemy Within."

The speculation regarding the "guest villain" of *Star Trek II* ended November 27, 1981, when an article in *The New York Times* revealed that Ricardo Montalban would appear in the film.

Although most *Star Trek* fans realized that Khan Noonian Singh would make a fine feature film villain, it was known that Montalban was extremely busy in his role as "Mr. Roarke" on the TV series *Fantasy Island*. News of his return to the *Star Trek* universe, in the person of one of the most intriguing personalities ever featured in the *Star Trek* television episodes, was enthusiastically received among the fan community.

Now that the question of the villain was answered, there were other worries on the minds of *Trek* fans. First and foremost was the question of whether or not Mr. Spock would die in the film. Beginning in October, 1981, rumors about this stunning possible turn of events circulated among the fan community. (This topic is covered elsewhere in this book.)

Also heavy on the minds of Trek fans was the list of people working on the film. Gene Roddenberry, *Star Trek*'s creator, was listed as the production's executive consultant. Executive producer Harve Bennett was familiar to *Star Trek* fans due to his association with *The Six Million Dollar Man, The Bionic Woman* and other television series. The name of producer Robert Sallin was *not* known. What kind of a *Star Trek* movie would these individuals produce? This was a matter completely open to speculation.

Director Nicholas Meyer, however, was familiar to science fiction fans, having made his directorial debut with *Time After Time*, a film well regarded within the science fiction community. But did he, like the others involved in the production, know anything about *Star Trek*? Would there be any concern about keeping within the existing parameters of the *Star Trek* universe?

Many fans of *Trek* reached the conclusion that, since Mr. Spock was rumored to die in the film, efforts to remain faithful to

Ricardo Montalban as Khan Noonian Singh, archenemy of Admiral Kirk

earlier *Star Trek* productions had been abandoned. They were wrong; fidelity to the original Star Trek was a vital concern of the new team.

In the heady days following *Star Trek II*'s release, Edward Egan, the film's unit publicist, mused on Harve Bennett's emotional involvement with the film: "Harve is really the one who is the whole reason for this film, and the sort of spirit behind it . . . ."

Egan also spoke of director Nicholas Meyer's commitment to the film and to the *Star Trek* mythos:

He . . . really fell in love with it. He told me he had never seen a whole episode on television until he was assigned the task of directing it. Then he sat down and had to watch, and he really did fall in love with the characters.

Producer Robert Sallin remembers that, previous to his involvement with *Star Trek II,* his experience with *Trek* was present:

> . . . Not in any great detail. I had of course watched episodes over the years when it first came out. . . . I was not really a committed fan. . . . I always felt, as Harve did, that we had to pay homage to the tradition, because after all that is what *Star Trek* is all about, but not to become slavish to it. . . .

Star Trek's fans, of course, had no way of knowing at this stage of the production that the makers of the film were worried about maintaining the same values in the movie that *they* were so concerned about.

On February 22, 1982, more speculation arose when *Time* magazine printed the first photograph ever to be published from *Star Trek II.* It showed Khan flanked by two young, pretty women. All were dressed in attractively tattered clothing. Khan looked extremely determined to do something, probably an action directed against Admiral Kirk. Here was confirmation that Khan, in the person of Ricardo Montalban, would indeed be appearing in the film. But the article described Khan as being "a villainous android."

Android, huh? What could this mean? Maybe this was a reconstruction fabricated by the original Khan to wreak vengeance against Kirk. Perhaps the makers of the film were changing the story of Khan to suit the needs of their script. Or maybe, which later seemed more likely, the writer of the piece was told that Khan was an android by someone who didn't know what the term meant; or the writer, knowing an android is a "synthetically made man," and knowing that Khan was a product of "genetic engineering," assumed that Khan was an android.

In the midst of all this speculation, it was still not even definitely known whether or not all the familiar faces from the *Enterprise* would be returning to appear in this movie. The papers were very definite in mentioning that William Shatner, Leonard Nimoy and DeForest Kelley had already signed for the film, but most newspaper and magazine articles followed these names by adding ". . . and other stalwarts of the original cast." The word *other* does not mean *all*. If not all, then who was missing from the new cast? Only time would tell if, indeed, anybody was missing and whether or not the film would live up to the fans' expectations.

All the doubts were not the exclusive domain of the fans. As is the case with every motion picture produced, there was no guarantee that limitless crowds would go to see the movie. The filmmakers and the studio that would distribute the finished product were just as worried as to the marketability of the product as the fans were concerned about its content. Actually, both the worries amounted to the same, because if the fans did not go back repeatedly to see the film, it would not make as much money as possible.

One individual who was caught between the concerns of Paramount and those of the *Star Trek* fans was Edward Egan, the unit publicist of *Star Trek II*. To Egan, it was apparent that everyone concerned wanted the best for *Star Trek II*. Fans and studio personnel alike wanted the film to be a success. Egan sums up the majority of the correspondence he received on the film and recalls how seriously the fans worried about the production:

> . . . Dreadfully seriously! The odd thing is that they think they own *Star Trek*. They think that since *they* saved the series from being cancelled, it then became theirs; that they can dictate whatever they want. I think that sometimes they don't consciously realize the movie company called Paramount Pictures . . . makes these things and is trying to make money by them, and we'd never do anything that *they* thought wouldn't make money. And when I would say, "Look, trust us, we're not going to mess this up, it'll be fine, wait until June fourth," they just refused to listen. . . .

It is a tribute to the *Star Trek* format that *Trek* fans take the series as seriously as Egan describes. And it is a tribute to everyone concerned with *Star Trek* that the motion picture *Star Trek II: The Wrath of Khan* is so completely pleasing to its creators and fans alike.

The Death of
Mr. Spock

The First Rumors

One day early in October, 1981, Leonard Nimoy walked along a street in a large city in China. He was there to complete his work in the television miniseries, *Marco Polo*. The actor was undoubtedly thinking about his dialogue, as well as the beauty of the city, when his eyes focused upon a newsstand. One of the publications facing him was the current issue of *The Wall Street Journal*. And there in front of him, halfway across the world from his home in California, was a picture of his features adorned with the special costume, hairdo and makeup of Mr. Spock. The headline read: "Does Mr. Spock Die In The Next Episode of 'Star Trek' Saga?" This was the first Mr. Nimoy heard of the question that would spark a storm of worry, doubt and protest initiated by individuals concerned about the fate of a friend.[1]

The natural assumption of the fans, once the rumor of the Vulcan's impending death became widespread, was that if Spock were killed, he would remain dead. In reality, this is usually the case. In science fiction, as spokesmen for the movie pointed out, it ain't necessarily so.

Concerned parties, distressed over the news, apparently did not recall that in the *Star Trek* television series, two recurring characters, Dr. McCoy and Mr. Scott, died and were restored to life by the advanced scientific techniques available to individuals

21

within each respective episode. McCoy, run through by the lance of the black knight in "Shore Leave," was undeniably dead but emerged unscathed at the episode's end. Scotty, attacked by Nomad, "The Changeling," was pronounced dead by McCoy, an expert at pronouncing others dead, and likewise was restored to life.[2]

In addition to assuming that Spock would permanently be reduced to a memory, some fans also concluded that Leonard Nimoy was the person to whom they should address their grievances. Edward Egan recalls:

> . . . There was talk of boycotts, and so forth. Leonard was getting hate mail, really vicious stuff, really uncalled for and most of it directed at him.

When asked if he took any of the mail personally, Mr. Nimoy recalled:

> I didn't take it personally. I just felt it was a rather narrow attitude on the part of some people of what their *Star Trek* should be, and to what extent they should determine what *Star Trek* should be. That's all . . . not a personal thing.

Leonard Nimoy elaborated on his feelings about the more vehement feedback received regarding Spock's death:

> I was saddened by it. Mostly I felt sad because I felt that there was a small, vocal group of people who were taking it upon themselves to dictate artistic choices. I really saw it as an artistic choice . . . an opportunity to explore something; to explore a perhaps frightening idea, but nevertheless to explore. And in a strange kind of way, what made me sad was that's what *Star Trek* is supposed to be about . . . about exploring strange and frightening situations. To boldly go, you know. And I thought the irony of it really saddened me. I thought these people, who claim to be the super *Star Trek* followers are in essence dictating, trying to prevent or arguing against exploration, and taking it upon themselves to

Leonard Nimoy: Mr. Spock. Star Trek fans everywhere express concern at rumors of his death.

decide what would be good, what would be bad, what would work and what wouldn't, what would be acceptable and what wouldn't.

The article in *The Wall Street Journal* also included quotes from an East Coast *Star Trek* fan, an articulate individual who was so concerned with the question of Spock's life or death that she and a dozen other fans (all women professionals, it was noted) got together and did research, then took out a quarter-page ad in a film industry trade publication with the headline "Why is Paramount deliberately jeopardizing $28 million in revenues?" This figure was based upon the projection that many *Trek* fans would not see the film a second time if Spock died, and that his death would also lessen profits of the movie's home-video sales.[3]

Paramount's public reaction to the ad, also spoken of in the *Journal* article, was to be glad that fans could care about the issue so much that they would spend the money that paid for the ad.

Leonard Nimoy recalls his reaction to the research and the ad:

. . . I'm sure you know about the research that was done by the lady in New Jersey, the one who ran the ad in the trade paper. I never spoke to her. I think she's a well-intentioned lady and I don't think she would just blindly make up figures and say, "This is the result of my research." I think she really did some kind of exploration or investigation, but it was so strange if you stop and think about it. Among other things, she laid out a kind of graph of how many people would see the picture more than once if Spock didn't die, and how many would see the picture more than once if Spock did. Well, the only analogy I can draw is . . . It's like standing outside of a record store. A person goes in and buys an album they haven't heard yet, and you say to them, "How many times are you going to listen to that album?" Of course you don't know until you've heard it, or seen the movie. You don't know. I found that funny.

Alternate Endings?

One other puzzling disclosure in the *Journal* piece asserted that even the highest-ranking people at Paramount might not know Spock's final fate. This brings us to the next phase of the events surrounding the death of Mr. Spock.

Almost two months later, a New York paper reported that due to increasing pressure prompted by huge amounts of mail, Paramount had "agreed to change" the ending of *Star Trek II*. An unnamed Paramount source was quoted as saying, "They have decided to shoot two (or more) alternate endings."[4]

Was there ever any official intent on the part of Paramount to foster the rumor that an alternate ending had been written and filmed for *Star Trek II*? The answer is no. The position of the Paramount executives, as recalled by producer Robert Sallin, was that they were in favor of releasing no information at all on this phase of the production.[5] Unit publicist Edward Egan confirms that at no time did he state there was more than one ending for the film. Executive Consultant Gene Roddenberry, speaking before a college audience before the film's release, specifically stated that he had seen only script pages involving one ending, and that he had no reason to think there was another.

If Paramount contributed to this rumor at all, it was only by refusing to divulge the ending of the film. The prints screened to get the film booked into theaters in advance ended abruptly at the point where Khan activated the Genesis Torpedo. This complete secrecy was also coupled with a direct reference to Spock appearing in the next *Star Trek* feature (if, in fact, there was to be one).

Early in May, 1982, the New York *Daily News* carried a short piece pertaining to *Star Trek II* in which Leonard Nimoy was quoted as not being worried about the question of Spock's death. The actor stated that he had no idea of how the film would actually "deal with the Spock question," and confirmed that he had already been approached about appearing in the next *Trek* film. Concerned parties could read the article in any of three ways: (1) as an indication that Spock would not die, (2) that even if he did die it was possible the character would return, or (3) that more than one ending existed, so the talks with Mr. Nimoy were based upon the studio using the ending in which the Vulcan lives.[6]

Most fans chose to believe that Spock would not die, and due to the disclosures that he *would* get killed in the film, they tended to believe that more than one ending existed. It was a logical conclusion, logically arrived at, as Spock would say. But it was determined without knowing all the facts, an act which the Vulcan would not have approved.

Newsday reported in a May 11 item that Spock indeed dies in the movie. The story quoted a Paramount executive as stating that some fans were crying after the first public screening of the movie, and that "No one ever dies in science fiction." *Newsday* also said a studio publicist (unnamed) assured them the ending of the film ". . . might be changed before it is released nationally June 4."[7]

If Spock died in the film, why did only *some* fans cry upon seeing this traumatic occurrence? Was it possible that some had seen one ending, and others another? And what was that other comment about nobody ever dying in science fiction? Not to mention the possibilities in the article's final statement. It certainly appeared that more than one ending to this film existed.

In actuality, everyone at that historic first showing in Missouri saw the same print; this was the same print as the released version of the film except for subtle differences in the technological perfection of some sequences.[8] What caused the varied reactions was the panning sequence on the Genesis Planet's surface.

In a sense, this idyllic look at Spock's casket, drifted safely to rest on this life-filled young world, can be said to be the alternate ending everyone was hoping for. Added very late in the film's production, this scene, combined with Kirk's reflections about returning here to make sure of what has become of his friend, provided more than the hint of hope for Spock that fans were hoping to see.[9] It is especially welcome after just having watched Spock's death scene and funeral for the first time.

The Death Scene

Spock's death scene is particularly potent to fans because of the circumstances that lead up to it. We see the setup, as Spock silently backs out of the bridge just as unobserved as Clark Kent usually is when leaving a room in the midst of a crisis. But unlike Kent, Spock is not invulnerable. On the contrary, he has always been extremely vulnerable, for all his pose of unemotionalism. We know exactly where he's going, what he'll probably do when he gets there . . . and we are also quite powerless to stop him. It is as if the Vulcan administers his neck-pinch to all of us, saying he has to do this for the good of everyone.

The way the scene is played, edited and scored all help to bring it across to the most intense degree possible. Spock's a staple to *Star Trek,* we keep telling ourselves; he *can't* die, but somehow we know he will. Or do we?

Once in the reactor room, the audience is very carefully manipulated. In the past, on the television *Trek* episodes, we have seen that Spock has various built-in defenses against a variety of things that would be harmful to others. He survived the poison thorns in "The Apple," the presence of the murderous creatures of "The Man Trap" and "Obsession" and the flying parasites of "Operation: Annihilate." Can he, we ask ourselves hopefully, survive this? Just as we do whenever we read or see *Romeo and Juliet,* or *A Tale of Two Cities,* we think *Maybe there's a chance!* Edward Egan reflects upon the scene:

. . . You're told in the reactor room that Spock is dead. . . . Scotty says he's dead already, and then you go over there, and you see that in fact he's *not* dead, and we're given this hope that he's going to be okay. And then, of course, we have to watch him die.

In "Operation: Annihilate" we saw a temporarily blinded Mr. Spock collide with a wall. In the reactor room scene, we see a similar collision and think that this, like the other, is some temporary difficulty . . . one which the Vulcan will survive. The hopeful illusion is strengthened by Spock's straightening out his jacket as he rises to address Kirk. Why would a dying man bother with a detail like this?

Leonard Nimoy offers some personal insight regarding these dramatic moments:

> It's a fascinating scene. There are a lot of interesting elements in that scene. The straightening of the jacket just came by instinct. That's the kind of actor I want to be. I want to find the things that come by instinct once I'm inside the character. And that's the kind of choice that you would never arrive at intellectually. You say, well, Spock gets up and he walks towards where Kirk is . . . but as I was standing I was thinking to myself. In a flash, this thought went through my head. I am now, for the last time, going to speak to my superior officer. One must be in order to do that. One must get one's self together to do that. It just went like a flash. I didn't plan to do it; it happened. It was a very moving experience for everyone on the stage, the shooting of that whole scene.

Motion pictures, however, are complex things. They are so completely planned in advance that only occasionally is an actor permitted the luxury of small improvisations. Would Mr. Nimoy's gesture be reshot? Happily, it wasn't thrown out:

> Once I had done it, I felt very right about it, and if anyone had suggested that I not do it again, I would have argued the point . . . and I don't remember having to argue the point. I was concerned about whether or not it would stay in the picture. It could easily have been cut out. I was very gratified to find out that it did stay in the picture.

Witnessing Mr. Spock's death, no matter how impermanent we hope it will turn out to be, is the Kobayashi Maru test for every *Star Trek* fan who sees the picture. We take it along with James T. Kirk. Most of us, like Kirk, accept the event as a reality, and the loss as something we must cope with if we are to continue to derive emotional and entertaining benefits from *Star Trek*. As is the case with Kirk, for us it is not anything but a reluctant acceptance. Should Spock somehow be restored to the *Star Trek* universe, and therefore to us, we would accept him back happily.

We've seen it before so many times in other forms of entertainment. In one of the most widely read books of all time, Jonah voluntarily casts himself overboard into the stormy sea to save all his shipmates. In classic literature, one man sacrifices himself to save an entire family in *A Tale of Two Cities*. In countless war movies we hear the equivalent of "That crazy kid— he stole the plane and took off without me!" as an impulsive young pilot heads alone toward the enemy to save his helpless squadron.

In all these other instances, however, we know that death is a border that can be crossed only once. The beauty of dealing with matters of science fiction is that borders are defined only by the limits of the authors' imaginations within this realm of future possibilities. That we can accept Spock's death is a passing grade in the Kobayashi Maru scenario. That we may expect the Vulcan to return is a tribute to the flexibility and hope inherent in science fiction.

Space Seed

SPOCK: It would be interesting, Captain, to return to that world in a hundred years and to learn what crop has sprung from the seed you planted today.

KIRK: Yes, Mr. Spock, it would indeed.

These words brought the *Star Trek* episode "Space Seed" to a close. Spock's comments proved extremely prophetic, although it took less than a hundred years to return to the planet Ceti Alpha V. Ironically, it was the Vulcan's statement that prompted the evolution of *Star Trek II*'s story, which includes the death of Spock.

Star Trek II: The Wrath of Khan could not have existed in its finished form without the initial introduction of Khan Noonian Singh presented in "Space Seed." The episode itself went through its own evolution, too.

There were at least two drafts of the story outline for "Space Seed." The chief difference between the two is the name of the central character: "Thornwald" in one and "Harold Ericcson" in the other. The story was originally very different, although its main events roughly matched those seen in the finished episode.

The outline discussed how individuals are products of their times and proposed that at some time in the near future criminals would be exiled from Earth in penal ships in much the same way as British criminals were once loaded onto ships and sent to colonize far shores. The only detail that survives intact from this stage of the story is the name *Botany Bay*.

Ericcson (or Thornwald) was a notorious, cold-blooded criminal exiled from Earth aboard a deportation vessel together with 99 other criminals and a volunteer crew of a few guards. All personnel were placed in suspended animation, with the guards' units set to revive them first.

An accident during the voyage resulted in Ericcson and some of his men being reawakened soon enough to overpower most of the guards and kill them. When the *Enterprise* discovered the sleeper ship, skeletons provided evidence that there had been a struggle of some sort. Attempting to discover what had happened, Kirk found Ericcson and was promptly assaulted by the man. All the survivors, including Ericcson, were removed and deposited in the *Enterprise* brig. There was one exception: the one remaining guard, ill and unconscious, was taken to sickbay.

Kirk now knew Ericcson was aggressive and probably criminal, but he still did not know the full truth. To prevent the Captain from learning everything, the desperate Ericcson escaped from the brig and murdered the unconscious guard, then slipped back into the brig.

To Marla McGivers, Ericcson was a daring rogue reminiscent of the ancient, hot-blooded individuals romanticized by history. As in the final version of the tale, she fell for him like a ton of bricks. She had no idea of just how cold-blooded he could be when it came to the act of murder.

It was Ericcson's intention to take over the *Enterprise* and become a pirate, raiding freighters and making his people rich. With Marla's help, he captured the starship and would have kept it, except for one detail. As desperate a criminal as he was, Ericcson had fallen in love with Marla. When he had the opportunity to kill Kirk in a phaser fight, Marla got between the two adversaries. Rather than see her injured, he surrendered to Kirk.

The episode had other differences from the finished episode. The *Botany Bay* of the outline left Earth in the year 2096 and traveled through space for 500 years before the *Enterprise* found her. The story's author also depicted the Earth of the near future as severely overpopulated, resulting in the establishment of "seed ships" to eliminate the criminal element.

The storyline was okayed and became a first-draft script (dated December 7, 1966), which in turn evolved into a final draft (dated December 8), a revised final (December 12) and finally a second revised final (dated December 13, 1966).

By the time of the last revision, Ericcson had evolved into Khan Noonian Singh, the genetic superman.

"Space Seed" makes it clear that Khan is an exceptional individual, a product of selective breeding growing out of the "Eugenics War" of the 1990s. After his initial narrow escape due to his failing unit, Khan proceeded to startle Dr. McCoy with his "amazing physical and recuperative power." Referring to Khan as he lay half conscious in sick bay, McCoy marveled, "There's something inside this man that refuses to accept death. . . . Even as he is now, his heart valve action has twice the power of yours or mine. Lung efficiency 50 percent better."

These characteristics account for Khan's superior strength. "I'd estimate he could lift us both with one arm," McCoy continued. "It'll be interesting to see if his brain matches his body." Unfortunately, Bones was correct in his suspicions regarding Khan's potential. He mastered the ship by reading the technical manuals that Kirk naively permitted him to study and almost succeeded in mastering Kirk as well. He neatly evaded Kirk's questioning sessions, counting on McCoy to testify to his relatively depleted condition. He could not, however, escape from Spock's probings. Using the *Enterprise* computer, the Vulcan made some interesting discoveries. "I've collected some names, made some counts . . . by my estimate, there were some 80 or 90 of these young supermen unaccounted for when they were finally defeated."

And later he pegged Khan Noonian Singh as "From 1992 through 1996, absolute ruler of more than a quarter of your world from Asia through the Middle East."

Even Kirk seemed to echo Marla's admiration of the man: "He was the best of the tyrants . . . and the most dangerous. They *were* supermen in a sense. Stronger, braver, certainly more ambitious, more daring . . ."

At the climax of the episode, Kirk faces Khan for the inevitable personal battle between them. "I have five times your strength," Khan warns the Captain. But just as the supermen had been created by scientists who forgot that "superior ability breeds superior ambition," Khan foolishly threatened to destroy the *Enterprise,* forgetting that Kirk might somehow find the strength to defeat him if the thing he loved the best was in danger.

Throughout "Space Seed," although Khan was clearly a conquerer ("Such men dared take what they want"), it was clear that he did not fancy himself to be a criminal. To him, it was logical that since his was the superior mind, *he* should rule. He had no wish to become an Errol Flynn–type pirate, only to rule as was his due.

Khan is a thoroughly charming individual in the episode and in the motion picture as well. In "Space Seed" he makes it clear that he respects Kirk as an individual, despite his frankness, observing, "Captain, although your abilities intrigue me, you are quite honestly inferior. Mentally, physically. In fact, I am surprised how little improvement there has been in human evolution."

He has no wish to kill Kirk, has no hatred for the man. At one point, as the Captain is suffocating in the ship's pressure chamber, Khan observes that his death is ". . . so *useless.*"

His final defeat comes about in the episode as the result of his emotional attachment to Marla McGivers. Trusting her, and believing her to be completely won over to his side, it does not occur to him that her reasoning regarding the Captain's death would not match his own, to the extent that she would successfully take steps to save the Captain's life. Kor, the Klingon, would probably say, "Foolish, foolish man. He should have killed the woman at his earliest convenience after taking over the ship." But what do Klingons know of love or trust or loyalty? Khan's life is ruled by these characteristics. Despite his superior abilities, and his superior ambitions, Khan Noonian Singh is essentially a likeable and honorable man.

Kirk, realizing that a man like Khan would probably have languished and died in a Federation rehabilitation facility, acknowledged that he recognized Khan's positive traits. Rather than force him into useless captivity, Kirk decided to force the man to channel his survival instincts to good use—the taming of a world. By this reasoning, although he was, of course, completely unaware of it, he was condemning his friend, Spock, to death years later. But that's another story . . . one that is wonderfully covered in *Star Trek II: The Wrath of Khan.*

The Earliest Drafts

The Beginning

On November 13, 1980, a Paramount Pictures interoffice communication was sent to Gary Nardino, president of Paramount Television. The sender was Harve Bennett. The subject of the memo was the motion picture then entitled *Star Trek: The Movie II,* a project being prepared by the studio's television arm, with Mr. Bennett as executive producer. The memo, the earliest known correspondence relating to the storyline of the film, read as follows:

Dear Gary:

Per your request, I am enclosing my first thumbnail sketch of the story I have proposed for the next *Star Trek* feature. Though brief, I think it includes all areas I feel essential to the project.

Regards,
Harve

This was the beginning of a complex creative process involving many individuals, inspired and helmed by Harve Bennett. The final result would be the motion picture *Star Trek II: The Wrath of Khan.*

Along the way of this production's evolution, ideas would come, go and change. Characters would be introduced, rewritten, dropped or expanded upon. And this would all happen within a prescribed deadline, a preset budget and an unwavering respect for the elements and individuals that constituted the original *Star Trek* format.

Bennett's initial story began as Admiral James Kirk sat behind a desk on Earth performing his Starfleet duties. News of a colonial rebellion on a Federation planet reached the Admiral who, instead of dispatching a starship to restore order, took command of the *Enterprise* and proceeded to the trouble spot himself. The reason for his personal attention on this mission was a woman whom Kirk had always loved.

On his way to the planet, Kirk rescued a drifting spacecraft, aboard which was the woman he loved. The son who resulted from the love affair between Kirk and the unnamed woman was now a leader of the revolution.

The young rebels, in their puzzling attempt to change their government from a democracy to a unique form of dictatorship, had taken hostages. A confrontation between them and the starship was inevitable. The confrontation resulted in Kirk's being captured and sentenced to death by his own son, who had just met him for the first time.

Before Kirk could be executed, however, the revolutionaries were attacked by the rebellion's true instigators. These inhabitants of the neighboring world, Ceti Alpha V, were a group of twentieth-century superhuman products of genetic engineering, led by Khan Noonian Singh. On stardate 3141.9,[1] the entire party had been exiled to the Ceti Alpha world by Captain Kirk after their unsuccessful attempt to commandeer the *Enterprise*.[2] Khan's purpose in fostering the revolution had been to create a situation from which to attack and conquer the United Federation of Planets.

As Khan and his people pressed their fight against everyone else, Kirk, his son, and the young revolutionaries united to combat their common foe and quell the threat to peace. During the fight they came to understand and trust each other.

The treatment ended with Kirk's son and the other young leaders electing to join the *Enterprise* crew and direct themselves at the challenges offered in outer space adventures and, as Mr.

Bennett mentioned specifically, ". . . Together, they will boldly go where no man has ever gone before."

No mention was made of other *Enterprise* principles in this treatment, not even of Mr. Spock and Dr. McCoy. Spock's death, therefore, was not mentioned, either. This does not necessarily mean that Spock's presence and/or death were not planned at this stage, as the only specific bits of action in the outline were those that directly figured in the situation regarding Kirk and his son and the defeat of Khan's plans.

Mr. Bennett subtitled this initial treatment "The War of the Generations." Elements from this version do survive in the film. In both places, Khan and his people are present. So are Kirk's lover of years ago, the son their relationship produced and the fact that the young man is distrustful of the Federation in general and Kirk in particular.

Collaboration

Shortly after this initial one-page storyline was written, Jack Sowards entered the creative picture. Sowards, a member of the Writers' Guild West, took Harve Bennett's ideas and expanded them into a nineteen-page outline with no title other than the generic "*Star Trek* Outline," dated December 18, 1980.

Sowards's expanded story included a two-page summary that explained how the United Federation of Planets had changed after the era depicted in the original *Star Trek* television episodes, and in *Star Trek: The Motion Picture*. According to this background, the original credo of the old-time explorers, "To Boldly Go Where No Man Has Gone Before," had been abandoned, and Starfleet had gone from exploration (and occasional brushes with the Klingon Empire and the Romulans) to simply protecting and developing the territories already within the sphere of the Federation.

This "freeze" on expansion has deeply influenced Admiral James T. Kirk. Like Spock, the outline indicated, Kirk had denied himself a part of his life. Spock inhibited his emotions; Kirk followed the rules and regulations of Starfleet and evaded lasting personal relationships. In line for the post of "Supreme Commander in Chief: Starfleet," he now found himself questioned by a younger, rebellious element that was challenging the totality to which he had dedicated his life. Because of this questioning, the introduction concluded, Kirk had also begun to question himself and, as Spock had in *Star Trek: The Motion Picture*, was looking for a meaning for his life.

The story opened on a peaceful planet within the Federation, where the Utopian society's youth was being instructed to revolt against their Federation masters by a mysterious, hooded individual called "The Teacher." Young David Kirk and his followers were promised weapons by the man on planet Omega Minori IV.

The scene then jumped to the starship *Enterprise,* where Captain Spock and first officer Baker witnessed one of the ship's warp engines damaged in an attack from an unknown vessel. In shutting the engine down, Spock was killed.[3] Hearing of Spock's death, Kirk transferred himself to the *Enterprise,* where he discovered that Baker, an admirer of his, was not running a tight ship. Kirk ordered the ship to proceed to Omega Minori IV at once. At that point, we were introduced to some new characters.

Science Officer Wicks, a male Vulcan[4] who was an advanced student of Spock's, first gave Kirk a difficult time, calling the Admiral illogical for expecting a Vulcan to understand a sense of humor.

O'Rourke, a female member of the bridge crew, also initially clashed with Kirk. The feeling was mutual, until he realized he was in love with her.

Requesting O'Rourke to play back the complete Captain's Log, Kirk also got a private playback of Spock's Personal Log, which contained an admission that Spock had decided, immediately before his death, to catch up on his previously disavowed emotions. The log was especially significant due to its reason for Spock's decision: his exposure to the massive mind of "V'ger."[5]

It was after hearing this admission of Spock's that the relationship between Kirk and O'Rourke was clarified.

Encountering a refugee ship from Omega Minori IV, the *Enterprise* rescued survivors including Diana, an old love of Kirk's. Here we run into another complication: Dr. McCoy is aware that Diana has a son—Jim's son, whom the Admiral knows nothing about.

After confronting Captain Baker and Mr. Wicks and warning them to run a tighter ship, Kirk visited the planet. There he heard conflicting reports about a peaceful revolution and a bloodbath. Attempting to decide which to believe, Kirk sent for a detachment of the Federation Marines.

Kirk realized there was indeed bloodshed but did not believe the rebels were to blame for it. David, on the other hand, initially thought Kirk and his people were responsible for the violence. Kirk ordered the *Enterprise* away from the planet, and David began to trust him and grow suspicious of The Teacher . . . suspicious enough, at least, to arrange a meeting between The Teacher, himself and Kirk.

Confronting The Teacher, Kirk dashed forward and ripped a concealing hood away from the figure . . . but there was nobody beneath the cloak. As the *Enterprise* sensors reported only two life forms in the area (Kirk and David), The Teacher's temple faded and transformed itself into a dark cavern,[6] within which Kirk was face to face with The Teacher, now revealed as Khan Noonian Singh.

Khan, while in exile, had learned to create illusions in the minds of others.[7] His attempts to subject Kirk to fatal illusions were unsuccessful, due to the Admiral's conviction that the resulting vacuum, fire and other effects were not real.[8]

Kirk and David, who had learned to trust each other, decided to venture together into outer space to explore once more.

Sowards was aware that the outline needed more definition and action, mentioning where additional interrelationships could appear and welcoming suggestions about what form the final chase and confrontation between Kirk and Khan should take.

The Next Step

There next appeared a six-page treatment entitled "New Outline," and bearing no byline or date. Divided into eighteen numbered divisions in its plot, the revised outline was getting closer to the final product and indicates that the author had done considerable homework in familiarizing himself with the *Star Trek* format, especially those portions that dealt with Khan.

This version began as Commander Terrell and Lt. Checkov *[sic]*, beamed down to Ceti Alpha V to check on whether Khan and his people had survived. If not, the lifeless world was to be used as the testing ground of a new weapon; if so, survivors would be removed to a different planet. We quickly learn that Khan was alive, that he possessed the power of creating illusions and that he wanted vengeance on Captain Kirk.

Creatures called Wee Beasties were introduced, and Terrell and Chekov were exposed to them. These creatures were more like the ones seen in the TV episode "Operation: Annihilate": they attached themselves to their victims' backs.

Back on Earth, Vice Admiral Kirk received a personal call from his old friend and ex-lover, Dr. Janet Wallace,[9] who said she could use a visit from an old friend. Bones then entered and reminded Jim that he wanted to go to see Captain Spock on the *Enterprise* before the ship left drydock (still more modifications).

Aboard the *Enterprise,* Spock was glad to see them and introduced Savik, his male Vulcan first officer, and Diana O'Rourke, the ship's librarian/historian. A relationship developed between the sharp and good-looking O'Rourke and Kirk. Kirk decided that he and Bones would accompany Spock on his mission to test a new weapon on Omega Minori IV.

Back on that world's Federation starbase, Commander Terrell claimed to have received orders that there would be no planetary test; that the weapon was instead to be used in an attack on the Klingons. Young David Wallace, leading a group of officers, protested. David took the weapon and hid it in the planet's desert region.

On the way to Omega Minori IV, the *Enterprise* was attacked by the Federation starship *Reliant* and caught without her shields up. An engine was damaged and Spock died while deactivating it, giving the relationship (as the outline's author pointed out) between Kirk and O'Rourke a chance to become more intense.

On Omega, Kirk angrily confronted his old friend Terrell, with whom he had attended the Academy thirty years before.[10]

Merritt Butrick as David and William Shatner as Admiral Kirk. Kirk's son David played an important role in early drafts of the movie script. His character and function were changed substantially in later versions.

Terrell then convinced Kirk that the starbase's young cadets had mutinied, stolen the Omega System (the weapon) and commandeered the *Reliant*. Kirk sent for the starship *Constitution* to quell the revolt. Although understandably hostile to the rebels, Kirk rejected Terrell's request to use the *Enterprise* phasers to stun the entire planet (except the starbase, insulated behind its shields). Hearing from Janet that David is his son and a leader of the revolt, Kirk arranged a meeting with David, who told him the real reason for the revolt. Kirk promised David that he would try to learn just what was happening.

Khan, monitoring the meeting, sent down soldiers and stole the Omega device from the rebel cadets.

Kirk, confronting Terrell, was forced to kill him . . . and witnessed the Wee Beastie. When another creature left Chekov, Savik captured it and later determined its origin was Ceti Alpha V, which led to Kirk's suspecting the presence of Khan.

Kirk, attempting again to meet with the rebels, was then captured by them and, because they thought him responsible for stealing the Omega device, sentenced to death. Janet, however, arrived and told David he was Kirk's son; shocked, David began to trust Kirk.

Khan attempted to defeat Kirk by filling his mind with various illusions, including the image of the two squared off, fighting a duel with rapiers. For a short time, Khan's illusion threatened to cause Kirk's death. Khan callously ran Kirk through the heart, but the Admiral survived because he knew the weapon was purely imaginary.[11]

The *U.S.S. Constitution* arrived and was blown up by Khan, using the Omega weapon, which cancelled out the starship's shields.

Savik, however, came up with an effective battle strategy, and after Scotty, the chief engineer, repaired the damages to the *Enterprise* the ship was able to foil the low-velocity Omega projectiles. Khan's vessel was destroyed in an explosion perceived on sensors throughout the galaxy.[12]

Kirk sent an all-channel message to all concerned, including the Klingons and Romulans, explaining that the explosion was simply a test of a new Federation weapon,[13] and the outline concluded with Kirk and David realizing they had much to learn from each other. Perhaps they could stay together and explore the universe in addition to each other's personalities.

The Plot
Thickens

On February 20, 1981, a very significant script draft was completed. The title was *Star Trek: The Omega System* and the writer was Jack Sowards. The script had been developed from his outline of December 18, 1980. The same characters featured in that outline are in this expanded version, and here they begin to have still greater resemblances to their later-draft selves.

The scenes between Kirk and McCoy are well developed, making maximum use of the doctor's cynicism. Kirk is a desk-bound Vice Admiral. Uhura is his administrative assistant. When Kirks asks McCoy "How are you?" the doctor's response is, "The question is . . . How are YOU? Plowing through the stormy seas of bureaucracy, day after day. . . . When was the last time you had your blood pressure checked?"

Also present in this draft is Savik, who at this point is still a male, apparently evolved from the previous outline's "Mr. Wicks." It is more than implied that Savik has emotional tendencies and capabilities.

In this version of the script there is some effective interplay involving Kirk and Spock, but by page 45 of the script (approximately one-third of the way through the story), the Vulcan dies under the same circumstances as those of the previous outline (not that far removed from the way he ultimately meets his death in the final version).

The O'Rourke character is still present as the chance for Kirk to catch up on his poorly pursued personal life. For the most part,

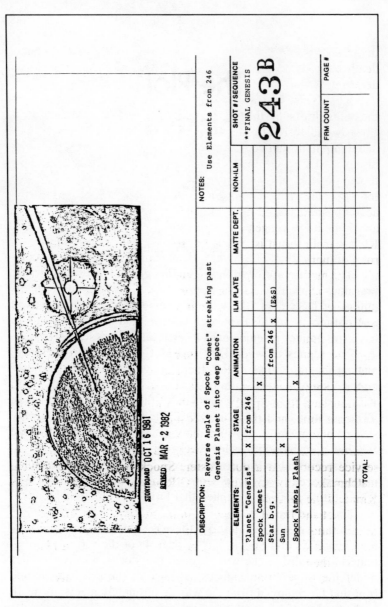

A storyboard charts the course of Spock's burial torpedo. The shot was filmed differently when the ending of the movie was changed to make the Vulcan's ultimate fate more ambiguous.

their relationship is held in the background, for after Spock's death Kirk cannot spare time for personal matters until he has determined why the *Reliant* attacked the *Enterprise*.

Khan's role is still very much in the background compared to the final drafts of the script. He uses the Beastie-controlled Chekov and Terrell to rule the starbase that houses the scientists and equipment that constitute the Omega System. Together with his wife, Marla, Khan plots from the sidelines, talking about how the Federation, the Klingons and the Romulans could all live together, united under his rule; there would be no end to the accomplishments, he says, and he is completely serious. There is an element of vengeance here, but because Marla still lives, Khan's main thrust is directed at restoring his former glory as a ruler of men.

The madness is apparent, though, as Khan also makes it clear that although he despises the notion, he will not hesitate to use the thousands of Omega missiles (four of which are enough to destroy a planet).

One touch that is missing from later drafts is an expansion upon the taped "last will and testament" that Kirk left for Spock and McCoy in the TV segment "The Tholian Web." This time around, Spock's message for Kirk is extremely wordy. It includes an admission from Spock that he has known he's been changing for some time, and that his exposure to V'ger was only a stop along the way. In his message, the Vulcan tells his friend Kirk not to throw his life away by disavowing his personal life in favor of a service record and a duty roster. Spock is in a sense playing matchmaker between Kirk and O'Rourke, as well as between Kirk and the *Enterprise*.

Janet and David Wallace, as in the outline, are again reduced to the status of rebels hiding in the caves. The caverns here were not caused by the Omega weapon; they are simply a place to conceal them.

There is some interesting interplay between Kirk, his son and his lover.

The communication between father and son grows most sober as Kirk, sentenced to death by the rebels, makes the final request that David be his executioner. This is merely a plot to talk

The Eden Cave as it finally evolved: a matte painting by Chris Evans

to David alone; Kirk may also be trying to force his son to trust him in what appear to be his last moments.

Kirk's emptiness and his feelings of growing old and obsolete are largely based, in this script, upon his regret at being alone, having no one to share his life with. This makes his dialogues with David and Janet all the more poignant.

In the final confrontation between Kirk, Khan and David, Kirk uses his considerable force of will to make David believe Khan's threats are not real.

In this draft, an interesting turn of events makes itself apparent for the first time; it will still be present in the film itself. During the days of the TV series, Kirk often turned his personal strength to the task of exorcising or helping someone else. In this situation, his strength is directed by McCoy at forcing him to help himself. Kirk hasn't thought this much about himself since the early adventure entitled "The Enemy Within."

With all the good moments in this draft, and with all the future promise this script suggests, it is still Khan who steals the show.

At one point, when David lies to him about the location of the Omega triggers, the villain responds: "If you're going to lie to me, I want to hear a great lie . . . a powerful lie . . . an overwhelming lie!"

As in the outline from which this first draft script has been taken, the story ends with Kirk and his son piloting the *Enterprise* together, searching for new worlds to understand, new adventures to experience together.

The next significant change is in another full script, this time designated a final draft entitled *Star Trek: The Genesis Project* and dated April 10, 1981.

In this draft, the Genesis Project is present almost in its full state of potential. The device in question is no longer simply a destructive weapon; the cave in which it is hidden was manufactured using a Genesis Torpedo.

Dr. Carol Baxter and her son David are almost fully evolved into their final forms, but something is still missing about them, and about most other elements of this script, too.

In this version, Mr. Spock lasts until page 66 (scene 95) and exits with a lengthy speech delivered through a plastic barrier, again very similar to the final version of his death. Appropriately, the Vulcan's last thoughts focus on how logical and well ordered the universe now seems to him.

Marla McGivers is still alive to keep Khan company throughout this story. The two are the last survivors aboard the *Reliant* and die together in the explosion that destroys the ship. There is a very warm relationship here between the two, with the running gag being Khan's question "Did I ever tell you that I love you?" "No." ". . . And I probably never will."

Khan, at this point, still possesses the power of projecting illusions into people's minds. The final confrontation between Kirk, Khan and David is very similar to the way it was presented in the earlier drafts.

At this point in the script's evolution we come to an interesting occurrence. Up until this time, Harve Bennett and Jack Sowards have been working together to firm up their script. Now, during the summer of 1981, an outside writer enters the picture, one not unfamiliar to *Star Trek* fans. An outline and a full script for

Rev. 10/30/81

STAR TREK: THE UNDISCOVERED COUNTRY

MAIN TITLE SEQUENCE (TO BE DESIGNED)

FADE IN:

1   IN BLACK   1

Absolute quiet. SOUND bleeds in. Low level b.g.
NOISES of Enterprise bridge, clicking of relays,
minor electronic effects. We HEAR A FEMALE VOICE.

                        SAAVIK'S VOICE
              Captain's log. Stardate 8130.3,
              Starship Enterprise on training
              mission to Gamma Hydra. Section 14,
              coordinates 22/87/4. Approaching
              Neutral Zone, all systems
              functioning.

INT. ENTERPRISE BRIDGE

As the ANGLE WIDENS, we see the crew at stations;
(screens and visual displays are in use): COMMANDER
SULU at the helm, COMMANDER UHURA at the Comm Con-
sole, DR. BONES McCOY and SPOCK at his post. The   *
Captain is new -- and unexpected. LT. SAAVIK is young
and beautiful. She is half Vulcan and half Romulan.
In appearance she is Vulcan with pointed ears, but her
skin is fair and she has none of the expressionless
facial immobility of a Vulcan.

                        SULU
              Leaving Section Fourteen for
              Section Fifteen.

                        SAAVIK
              Project parabolic course to
              avoid entering Neutral Zone.

                        SULU
              Aye, Captain.

                        UHURA
                    (suddenly)
              Captain... I'm getting something
              on the distress channel. Minimal
              signal... But something...

                        SAAVIK
              Can you amplify?

                        UHURA
              I'm trying...

                                          (CONTINUED)

Page one of the final script. Lt. Saavik is introduced, and the _Kobayashi Maru_ episode begins.

STORYBOARD MAR - 2 1982

(Description continued): (Flashing X-Y-Z cusor)
is at far end of zone. Aiminanumerics indicate
KOBAYASHI MARU Data in lower right.

DESCRIPTION: INT--ENTERPRISE VIEWSCREEN--Tactical display.
Computer Graphics show ENTERPRISE Navigaion Sphere at left
f.g. Travelling toward KLINGON Neutrality Zone against
simple starfield. KOBAYASHI MARU symbol (continued above)

NOTES:

ELEMENTS:	STAGE	ANIMATION	ILM PLATE	MATTE DEPT.	NON-ILM	SHOT #/SEQUENCE
Regular Viewscreen			X			**OPENING SIMULATOR
Computer Graphics			X E&S			
						2X
TOTAL:						
						FRM COUNT PAGE #

This storyboard from the opening sequence shows the *Enterprise*
viewscreen and the planned special effects. Every shot in the film was
carefully storyboarded.

Kirstie Alley: Lt. Saavik, half Vulcan and half Romulan

The final logo for *Star Trek II: The Wrath of Khan*

Star Trek II were submitted. His outline was entitled *Star Trek: Worlds That Never Were* and was dated July 18, 1981.

"Worlds That Never Were" eliminates the characters of Khan Noonian Singh and Marla McGivers. We are instead introduced to two aliens, Sojin and Moray, from another dimensional plane. Sojin and Moray were linked together by a life force, communicated telepathically and added a great deal of unnecessary complication to the plot.

The rest of the plot elements in the outline all appear to be evolving toward the final film's content. Project Genesis is here in all its potential.

At the crucial moment of confrontation between Kirk and the aliens, the voice of the dead Spock is heard, and both Kirk and McCoy feel his presence. The implication is that he has, by unknown means, found his way back from death, apparently without the help of the Genesis effect.

One significant change that would carry through all the subsequent revisions is introduced here: Dr. Savik, for the first time, is described as a half-Vulcan, half-Romulan woman.

The script, developed from this outline, was entitled *The New Star Trek,* dated August 24, 1981. It contained the ideas from this outline and a few new ones as well.

It was, for instance, Spock's birthday instead of Kirk's. At one point, on the *Enterprise,* Captain Spock's crew assembled and sang "Happy Birthday" to him in Vulcan.

Spock, in this script, was more honest about his human condition than he was in the final drafts, admitting to Kirk just before he died, that "I understand, Jim . . . I've always understood."

The final screenplay by Jack B. Sowards evolved very quickly from this point in time under the title *Star Trek: The Undiscovered Country*.

Almost 25 sets of revised script pages were written between September 4, 1981, and April 14, 1982. Full scripts, each with the designation "Revised Final Draft" were produced, bearing the dates September 16, September 25 and October 5, 1981.

The final result, the blueprint for *Star Trek II: The Wrath of Khan,* gives the appearance of having evolved quickly. Careful readings of each script, each set of revised pages and each individual outline, however, reveal the constant stream of thought and sweat that actually produced the shooting script of the film.

The Cuts

The Revised Final Draft script for *Star Trek II,* written by Jack B. Sowards (story by Harve Bennett and Jack B. Sowards) is dated January 18, 1982. The interior pages assume a rainbow appearance, as they are pink, yellow, green, orange and other colors, each of which signifies a stage in the script's rewrites. The pages in this draft (which is entitled *Star Trek II: The Undiscovered Country*) bear revisions from September through November, 1981. As is the case with all motion pictures, all the scenes shot did not make it into the final cut of the film. Some appear in slightly different forms. A detailed accounting of these scenes' *original* forms follows.

As Kirk and Spock stood in the Academy corridor outside the Simulator Room, talking about the Admiral's unique solution to the Kobayashi Maru scenario, Spock observed that Kirk's answer to the problem would not have occurred to a Vulcan. (He does this without revealing the actual solution.) Kirk responded by noting that Saavik is both first-rate and emotional. Spock clarified Saavik's origins a bit by explaining, "She's half Romulan, Jim. The admixture makes her more volatile than—me, for example."

During the same scene, as Kirk and Spock were saying goodbye to each other, the Vulcan revealed that he had seen something was troubling his old friend regarding his current Earthbound lifestyle and the prospects of going back to an apartment that was not really home for him. "Something oppresses you," observed Spock. Kirk responded, "Something," and did not elaborate.

When Kirk received his birthday visit from Bones, Kirk accepted the gift of the spectacles without initially knowing what the odd device's purpose was. Dr. McCoy asked Kirk, "Why isn't there a girl up here?", hinting that his friend may have been passing up Terran entanglements because he was still too involved with his real love, the starship *Enterprise.*

On the surface of Ceti Alpha V, as Terrell and Chekov scouted around, Chekov was startled to see a child staring out of the porthole of Khan's quarters. The implication was that the child was Khan's, but all scenes with the baby were edited out of the finished film.

Inside the cargo hold on Ceti Alpha V, Khan had some additional dialogue that elaborated upon his hatred of Kirk:

On earth, two hundred years ago, I was a prince, with power over millions—now, like Prometheus, I have been left by *Admiral* Kirk to digest my own entrails.

And later:

And I'll wager he never told you about his shipmate, the beautiful and courageous Lieutenant McGiver, who gave up everything to join me in exile. OUT OF LOVE. And see how *Admiral Kirk* requited her devotion—she's dead as earth! A plague upon you all.

During the same scene, Khan lifted Terrell into the air, not Chekov.

On the *Reliant* bridge, as Kyle and Beach were worrying about what had become of their Captain and Chekov, Terrell informed his people that he was beaming up with guests.

On their way to the *Enterprise* in the shuttlecraft, Kirk thanked Sulu for the chance to be reunited with his original *Enterprise* bridge crew. During the same scene, Kirk took pride in telling his former helmsman that he would soon be commanding his own ship, the *U.S.S. Excelsior.* Kirk mentioned he had cut the orders himself and affirmed that Sulu had earned his promotion many times over.

Ike Eisenmann: Cadet Peter Preston, Commander Scott's nephew

In the interior of the *Enterprise* docking bay, just after Kirk had come aboard, Spock and Saavik conversed. This script has no indication that their conversation was taking place in the Vulcan language, and additional dialogue clarified Spock's role as Saavik's teacher:

> We can't all be perfect, Saavik. You must control your prejudices and remember that as a Vulcan as well as a Romulan you are forever a stranger in an alien land. Around you are humans, and as a member of the Starfleet you are unlikely ever to escape their presence or their influence. You must learn tolerance in addition to all else I have taught you. Tolerance is logical.

Soon afterward, in the engine room, there was more dialogue involving Kirk and Cadet Peter Preston. Kirk first puts one over on the youngster, kidding him about how many times he has listened to Scotty telling him his troubles, jokingly calling the *Enterprise* a "flying death trap," a situation that would later prove terribly accurate for the cadet. Preston retaliated to the rib effectively. In the most significant difference between this version of the scene and the way it finally appeared on film, it was revealed that Preston was Montgomery Scott's nephew, his sister's youngest child, "Crazy to get to space."

On the bridge of the *Reliant,* Khan had dialogue that referred directly back to "Space Seed," observing that the *Reliant* was ". . . Not much different from *Enterprise*. When I was a guest aboard her some years ago, Captain Kirk kindly allowed me to memorize her technical manuals."

Khan then forced the docile Chekov to reveal his knowledge of Genesis: he reported directly to Dr. Carol Marcus and Admiral Kirk definitely knew the details about the project.

Back on Regula, as Carol formulated the plans for the getaway of the Genesis staff, she observed their destination was ". . . for us to know, and *Reliant* to find out."

In the *Enterprise* turbolift, as Kirk and Saavik talked, the Admiral advised her to take the Kobayashi Maru test again, foreshadowing that soon *he* would have to take it again, without being able to change the program beforehand to save Spock's life.

As Khan delivered his ultimatum to Kirk, he again made reference to himself in allegorical terms. "I, Khan Noonian Singh, the eagle you attempted to cage forever."

As the crisis occurred in the engine room because of poisonous vapors released by the damage done to the ship, the crew chief ordered the cadets to turn on the blowers and clear out the noxious fumes. This entire scene was deleted.

As Dr. McCoy was frantically working to save Peter Preston's life, Kirk explained to Scotty that Khan didn't care who died so long as he could continue wreaking vengeance on the Admiral. Kirk also acknowledged that Peter's act of staying at his post prevented the *Enterprise* from being destroyed. This scene was originally much longer in other respects, too. Spock reported the impulse engines were restored, and Scotty said he would try to restore the main drive. Kirk and McCoy discussed how Khan could possibly have learned about Project Genesis. Finally, Kirk told McCoy that Khan had failed to destroy the *Enterprise* only because he knew something about the starship that Khan was unaware of.

When the bodies were discovered aboard the space station, the wanton nature of the slaughter was emphasized by Kirk's observation that even the galley chief was murdered, a man who probably knew nothing about Project Genesis.

After Chekov and Terrell were discovered, McCoy recognized Terrell, stating that he had once served with him. At that point he also theorized that Chekov and Terrell were suffering from a drug-induced brain disturbance. Terrell recognized McCoy, and when Kirk addressed Chekov he referred to him as "Pavel."

In the interior of the cavern, immediately after Kirk and company beamed down, Kirk was wrestled to the ground by David, who referred to him as a "dumb bastard" and announced that he was going to kill him. Carol then told him, "You do that and you'll have murdered your father."

Kirk, in this scene, was as startled as David. He had no idea he'd had a son, responding, "Carol. Is that true? Why didn't you tell me?" These events made Kirk appear naive rather than giving the impression that he'd known David was his son all along and had never made an attempt to see him.

David's first assumption was that it was Kirk and his people who had committed the slaughter on the space station. After learning that such was not the case, he was still extremely suspicious of Kirk due to his mistrust of the military . . . not to mention the shock of learning the "overgrown boy scout" was actually his father. Defensively, David denied this traumatic disclosure, stating that his father was a professor (apparently something his mother had led him to believe).

Carol, meanwhile, had discovered that being near Jim Kirk again meant perceiving him as a human being after years of looking at him as an undesirable presence. She noted he had acquired a few gray hairs.

While all this business would have meant additional insight into the individuals involved in the drama, it would also have slowed down the action that was to come.

When the action in this sequence started, it happened very

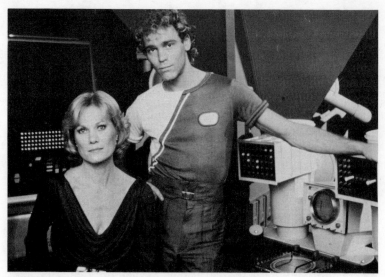

Bibi Besch (Dr. Carol Marcus) and Merritt Butrick (Dr. David Marcus). Much of the material associated with David's discovery of his father was eliminated from the final film.

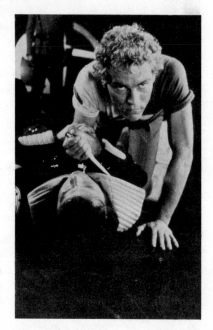

David's first meeting with his father. He assumes that Kirk is responsible for the murder of the scientists on Space Station Regula I. This shot was cut from the final film.

Merritt Butrick: Dr. David Marcus

quickly. We see David beginning to rush forward to try to prevent the Genesis Torpedo from being beamed aboard Khan's ship, but a short follow-up was edited out. Saavik, seeing David begin a foolish act that would probably have led to his death, actively held him back, remarking, "Only half of you would get there."

Also eliminated were some exchanges involving Kirk, McCoy, David and the sleeping Chekov. Bones confirmed that Chekov was alive, then dryly added to David, "You and your father can catch up on things." David also seemed to be dwelling upon the death of his friend, Jedda, having pushed Terrell's death into the background. McCoy, attempting to straighten out the young man's perspective, maintained the deaths were not the fault of Kirk, which David had implied. The men were killed "Because of you, son. You shouldn't have tried to rush someone holding a primed phaser. Anyway it isn't one man dead, it's two, in case you've lost count."

This revelation was followed by a period of silence, after which Kirk effectively changed the subject to food. It was next Kirk's turn to feel even more awkward as Carol described their son.

"He's a lot like you in many ways. Nothing I could do about it. He's smarter, of course; that goes without saying. Most of Genesis is really his."

One possible implication here is that life goes full circle; the life-giving Project Genesis was born from the minds of young people. Its physical presence, however, as everyone marveled over the beautiful interior of a formerly dead world, restored Kirk's elation over exploration. In the cave, he no longer felt old.

The actual reason for this trend of discussion, however, was the development of a relationship between David and Saavik. It was earlier implied that Saavik had altered her hairstyle for Kirk's benefit, appearing with him in a turbo-lift dressed in a less formal manner than usual. Producer Robert Sallin confirmed this when asked if such an intention actually existed.

"Yes, it was meant to be subtle. Another branch of a story which, if you'd allowed it to go, would get in the way."

Mr. Sallin also accounted for the decision, at that stage of production, to insert the beginnings of a relationship between Saavik and David, rather than between Saavik and Kirk.

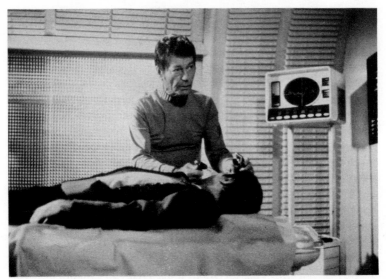

DeForest Kelley as Dr. McCoy operates on Chekov in sickbay aboard the *Enterprise*. The scene was dropped in the final film.

". . . As many young women would, she would realize that the older man might not be obtainable, and *look* who's here as a very reasonable substitute."

The actual exchange of dialogue, as David and Saavik sat together in the Genesis Cave, went like this:

DAVID: What are you looking at?

SAAVIK: The Admiral's son.

DAVID: Don't you believe it.

SAAVIK: Oh, I believe it. What are *you* looking at?

DAVID: I don't know.

Immediately after this exchange, Bones compares the place to the Garden of Eden, and Carol responds, "Only here, every apple comes from the Tree of Knowledge."

There was more pertaining to the fate of Mr. Chekov here, too. Earlier, McCoy had applied a dressing to the Commander's injured ear. In a subsequent scene, Kirk had changed the dressing, and back aboard the *Enterprise,* in the company of Carol and David, Bones worked on Chekov in sick bay.

As Mr. Spock ventures into the reactor room, he applies a Vulcan nerve pinch to McCoy. In this draft of the script, he did not transfer his hand to the mind-meld position and say, "Remember . . ." to McCoy.

After Mr. Spock's funeral, the scene of Kirk and company on the bridge was also longer, elaborating upon Kirk's perception of the seed of a relationship between Saavik and his son:

KIRK: I believe, you already know my, uh, son—Yes, well, why don't you show him around and . . .

SAAVIK: Aye, sir [to David]. So *you* turn out to be the dumb bastard. [They stare at her.] That is a little joke.

Saavik's joke referred to the earlier incident when David had pounced upon Kirk preparatory to stabbing him. The chances are that the audience would not have recalled the connection between these lines that late into the film. The entire exchange also diminished the feeling of reverence for the memory of Mr. Spock, which is uppermost in everyone's mind at this time in the film. Another deleted exchange of dialogue was between Bones and Carol Marcus as they both gaze at the viewscreen and the Genesis Planet:

BONES: . . . Will you look at that? Think they'll name it for you, Doctor?

CAROL: Not if I can help it. We'll name it for our friend.

Kirk, responding to Bones's question of how he feels, recites a line from Peter Pan. "Young. I feel young, Doctor. Lieutenant, new course: 'Second star to the right, and straight on till morning.' "

This draft of the script was written before the location shot of the Genesis Planet, which confirmed that Spock's casket had safely touched down on the new world. Kirk's intention to return, to seek out his friend, is therefore missing from this script.

There were a few other lines added to the screenplay after this stage of the script was written.

As Kirk, Bones and Saavik prepared to beam down to Regula, Spock asked Kirk to be careful. McCoy's retort of "*We will!*" was not yet inserted at this point.

Also added, as Kirk, McCoy and Spock view the Genesis tape proposal, was a line devised in conjunction with the implication (later added) that Spock's fate may not have been so final: "Genesis is life from lifelessness."

Certain scenes were also transplanted from where they were in this revised final draft to where they eventually are seen in the film's final cut. For example, the scene wherein Kirk faces the Cadets and explains how he's ". . . Going to have to ask you to grow up a little bit sooner than you expected," was originally seen *before* the scene in Spock's quarters. The scene in Kirk's apartment, which follows the conversation between Kirk and Spock in which Kirk mentions he'd headed home, was originally separated from the conversation by the first scene involving Chekov and Terrell aboard the *Reliant*.

It certainly would be interesting (even "fascinating") to see the full scenes delineated in this draft of the script. If such a print could be viewed, however, it would explain why the changes were made: to eliminate plot-line offshoots that would have diverted the audience from concentrating on the main problems at hand, and to tighten up the print so that the moments of excitement and decision would occur closer together, without these sidebars.

The Story

The *Star Trek* television series is filled with episodes that tell exciting stories and contribute valuable character insights. The episodes, though, were produced within standard television deadlines and standard television budgets. The series could never afford to depict the physical trappings of the *Enterprise* in as complete and complex a manner as the fans of the show had always wanted to see them. Due to the short length of each episode, and the deadline demands within which the scripts had to be written and revised, the same restrictions applied to the development of the story within each episode.

Star Trek II: The Wrath of Khan was, as is any motion picture, produced within very definite budget and time restrictions. These deadlines, however, allow much more time than TV deadlines. As a result, that much more of what we always wanted in the series is present in this motion picture. This is especially true of the story, which, although it is essentially an expanded television episode, permits much greater development of the plot and characters.

We are given as counterweights two extraordinary human beings: Admiral James T. Kirk and Khan Noonian Singh. Each is going through a crisis point in his life. Kirk, however, clearly has the better of the bargain. His two friends, Dr. Leonard McCoy and Captain Spock, are thoroughly a part of his life, and they are there to tell him exactly what his life needs. Tell him they do.

From sharing prior adventures with James Kirk, we know that his association with the starship *Enterprise* is an extraordi-

William Shatner: Admiral James T. Kirk

nary one. The responsibility of this huge ship deprives Kirk of being his own man. To a large extent, however, he finds it undesirable and impossible to be himself, to his fullest ability, without "her"—his ship. The *Enterprise,* he has stated in the past, ". . . is a beautiful lady, and we love her" ("I Mudd"). "I give, she takes . . ." is how he perceived "her" in "The Naked Time," adding that while he is the captain he can have ". . . no beach to walk on." In the same adventure, though, faced with losing command, he gazes up at interior bulkheads and states, ". . . Never lose you!" Even when he has attained his dream of settling down peacefully on an idyllic planet in "Paradise Syndrome," he still has dreams of ". . . The strange lodge that moves through the skies."

The obligations, the responsibilities, the power, the ability to get there and help (wherever "there" happens to be) are all necessities for Kirk if he is to remain alive.

Knowing this, *Star Trek* followers are in the same position as Spock and McCoy. We know that Kirk must get back to his *Enterprise,* as he has already begun to atrophy after relinquishing command to Spock. We are quite relieved when both Spock and McCoy say, in their respective ways, that Kirk *must* become captain of the *Enterprise* once again. We are even more relieved when he is back in the command chair again. And so, of course, is he.

Two questions arise regarding why Kirk does not have command of the *Enterprise* as the film opens. First, why did Kirk accept the position of admiral? The answer to this is known only to Kirk himself, but probably has to do with his midlife crisis. Second, if Spock is really Kirk's friend, why did he accept command of Kirk's ship? In the past, Spock had stated that command was not on his list of things to achieve. In "The Galileo Seven" he accepts the responsibilities of commanding a shuttle-craft and its crew but does not enjoy the occasion. Even in the upside-down universe of "Mirror, Mirror," Spock's parallel-dimensional self has no wish to become a starship captain (especially over in that plane; it's a high-risk job).

The most logical answer is that Spock, knowing the thought processes in his friend's head, is aware that sometime, hopefully soon, Kirk will strive to regain his old command. At that point, through Spock's efforts as captain, the *Enterprise* will again be there for Kirk to become a part of. Spock is "minding the store" for his old friend . . . babysitting, watching the old ship until its rightful commander can return.

Kirk returns in a most dramatic moment to solve one of the most potentially dangerous situations in Federation history. An old adversary, who has the advantage over Kirk in terms of both physical and mental strength, has the most potent device in the universe.

Fortunately for Kirk, Khan Noonian Singh's abilities are marred due to the man's madness. And who can blame him? He had built an empire back in 1996—97. He lost it all just as he was

Spock meditating in his cabin

on the verge, from his standpoint, of productively uniting the world under his rule. Rather than submit to capture, humiliation, imprisonment or worse, he leaves Earth with his faithful followers, all of whom have sworn allegiance to follow him in *any* undertaking, at *any* time (or *in* any time).

After a long, comfortable sleep, he awakens on the *Enterprise*. He attempts to take the ship, and almost wins . . but he makes one fatal error. He tells Kirk he will destroy the *Enterprise* and all aboard her. This Kirk cannot permit, and shortly after Khan has told him truthfully that ". . . I have *five times* your strength," Kirk beats him.

Once again, he has lost all his hopes but has obtained others. He has met, and fallen in love with, Marla McGivers. And he has a new world to win. Both these potential chances at happiness, however, are snatched from him. For him there is no *Enterprise* to command. But there *is* James T. Kirk to destroy!

Throughout all the action of the film, the personalities of Kirk and Khan are neatly balanced. Each raises his voice only once during the film; each is the epitome of a gentleman in his delivery. The one difference, of course, is that Khan tends to be extremely hostile and destructive due to the demands his madness makes upon him. Just as Kirk is obsessed with the *Enterprise,* Khan is obsessed with the idea of Kirk. Kirk, however, wishes merely to live his own life to the best of his ability. Khan wishes to remove everything that is dear to the life of Kirk.

This situation is the basis for the film's drama. In a bizarre manner, however, it also fills the requirements of classic comedy; or, more closely, of that staple of comedy known as "reciprocal destruction."

Reciprocal destruction reached a fine art in the hands of Laurel and Hardy at the Hal Roach Studios during the 1920s and 1930s. In its basic form, two individuals met, developed a profound hostility toward each other and sought to destroy everything important to the other person. It usually began with Oliver Hardy ringing comedy foil Jimmy Finlayson's doorbell. Before the sequence was over, Finlayson's clothes, his garden and virtually his entire house was a complete shambles. So was Hardy, his car and all the other things he had with him—all as the result of some simple misunderstanding or grating occurrence that got completely out of proportion.

In *Star Trek II,* Kirk does not start out wanting to destroy Khan, but Khan leaves him very little choice in the matter. In a detached sense, Khan displays the same eye-bulging indications of deep personal hostility as Finlayson did against Laurel and Hardy. Both individuals have a deep-seated need to achieve the destruction they try to generate.

The one important difference, of course, is that in Laurel and Hardy's universe no one every really got hurt. Cars, houses and individuals always returned completely intact after the laughs had been obtained at their expense. In *Star Trek II,* people, places and things are not so magically reconstituted without profound loss, adjustment and reconstruction.

There are numerous literary allusions in this film's script. Most of them revolve around the novels *A Tale of Two Cities* (written by Charles Dickens) and *Moby Dick* (written by Herman Melville).

A Tale of Two Cities is the source of such quotes as "It was the best of times, it was the worst of times . . ." and "It is a far, far better thing that I do now than I have ever done before . . ." The book, like the movie, culminates in one man sacrificing his life to save others.

Moby Dick is a study in obsession: the epic tale of Captain Ahab and his all-consuming hatred for the white whale responsible for the loss of his leg . . . and his sanity.

Khan Noonian Singh is Captain Ahab; Kirk is the subject of his hate. Just as Ahab permitted his ship to sink to get himself into a position to avenge himself upon the whale, Khan's ship is destroyed. And just as Ahab voluntarily drowned for the privilege of stabbing Moby Dick repeatedly with his harpoon, Khan activates the Genesis Torpedo with his dying breath. Khan's dialogue at this point in the film are the words that Ahab utters as the whale begins to dive, taking the sea captain to his doom: "To the last I will grapple with thee," and "From hell's heart I stab at thee . . . For hate's sake . . . I spit my last breath at thee!"

Moby Dick also features one of the most exotic characters ever to appear in an American novel: Queequeg, an ace harpoonist from a faraway tribe of cannibals. By performing a mystical ritual involving casting bones onto the deck of the ill-fated ship and "reading" their pattern, Queequeg knows that he will soon die . . . and proceeds to await his death with quiet dignity. In *Star Trek II*, by unknown means, Spock seems to have the same capability for forecasting his doom, which he prepares Kirk to accept by presenting him with the old edition of *A Tale of Two Cities*.

Star Trek II: The Wrath of Khan is, most of all, a story of the acceptance of loss, as expressed by the Kobayashi Maru test: the no-win scenario.

Khan Noonian Singh: a study in obsession (Ricardo Montalban)

Kirk, who has never actually coped with death before, must first realize that his youth is a thing of the past. He starts out by experiencing his midlife crisis, depressed because half his life is gone. He ends by realizing that half his life is waiting to happen, and that it can be just as exciting (or more so) than his previous experiences.

Both Kirk and McCoy must bear the loss of their friend Spock. Together these three formed one mind, with Kirk furnishing the impulse, Spock the logic and McCoy the modulation.

In the television episodes, we saw Kirk repeatedly devising solutions to dire threats. Many of these took the form of bluffs: the "corbomite devie" of "The Corbomite Maneuver," the "godfather" imitation in "A Piece of the Action," the harmless sugar pill of "Mudd's Women." All of these were really variations on "Hey . . . your shoelace is untied," on a colossal scale. And they have always worked. Kirk, as he confides to his son in this movie, has never actually taken the Kobayashi Maru test without changing the programming so that he can win; never, that is, until in communicating this fact to his son, Kirk realizes that he has just taken the test and passed, with flying colors.

Of the three principals, Spock has the best of times coping with his loss, although he loses the most . . . his life. As McCoy once pointed out to the Vulcan, Spock is not afraid to die because he's more afraid of living. Things have changed for Spock somewhat since McCoy's observation in the episode "Bread and Circuses," but Spock is still holding a good deal of his true self in check. He remains stoic and ready to defend his loyalties, obligations and friendships to the ultimate degree. It is unclear whether or not the Vulcan has a death wish, but it is painfully clear to us all by the end of the story that he is thoroughly prepared to die, as he has always been throughout the original *Star Trek* TV episodes. In "The Galileo Seven" Dr. McCoy could not believe that Spock was actually prepared to leave someone behind to die. Spock's answer at the time, to McCoy's observation that "Life and death are seldom logical," was "Attaining a desired goal always is!"

More than once in the series Spock demonstrated his willingness to die to protect that which he loved. He took the poison thorns meant for Kirk in "The Apple," risked death to obtain lifelong happiness for his ex-captain Pike in "The Menagerie" and subjected himself to unknown perils to kill the Beasties of "Operation: Annihilate." Spock is wrong; when it comes to himself, he has taken the Kobayashi Maru test several times and passed each time.

Khan passed the test, too, from his own point of view. When faced with the "no-win scenarios" in his life, he accepted his fate (while plotting how to undo the damage) until the last, when he attempted to take as many people with him as he could across the border that had become his final frontier: "the undiscovered country."

No matter how one chooses to look at the story of *Star Trek II,* one fact emerges above all others. It is a highly entertaining tale, filled with surprises, suspense and revelations. It is most assuredly an "audience participation movie" in the sense that it is like entering a huge, futuristic pinball game with all the inherent color, hard knocks and points to be scored. Perhaps this is why some *Star Trek* fans have reported difficulty in sitting through more than one showing at a time. This is not due to anything negative about the film—it's just a tiring movie to see because one not only watches it, one lives it as well. And that's what entertainment is all about!

Harve Bennett

Harve Bennett was born on August 17, 1930 in Chicago, Illinois. At the age of six, he began attending that city's Bradwell Grammar School. Five years later, he began his first active participation in the mass media as one of the regular contestants on the popular radio series *Quiz Kids*. Week after week, until 1946, young Harve answered the most difficult history questions, proving his mental mettle in preparation for his artistic and intellectual pursuits.

After finishing Chicago's South Shore High School, Bennett enrolled in the University of California, Los Angeles (UCLA). While there, he worked as a columnist on the staff of the Chicago *Sun-Times* from 1944–48, edited the "Archie" juvenile department store magazine and wrote several industrial films. It was at UCLA that Bennett first met classmate Robert Sallin, who would later become the producer of *Star Trek II*.

Graduating UCLA with a B.A. in theater arts and motion pictures, Bennett worked at other jobs before serving in the Army from 1952–55.

Upon his Army discharge, Harve became an associate producer for CBS Television, working both in Los Angeles and New York. Until 1960, he worked with such popular television entertainment figures as comedian Red Skelton, singer Frankie Laine and young Johnny Carson, who would later become a television superstar after succeeding Jack Paar as the emcee of the *Tonight Show* on NBC.

Harve Bennett, executive producer of *Star Trek II: The Wrath of Khan*

In 1958, Bennett became the producer of CBS' remote specials.

In addition to these projects, he also worked for the network as a freelance writer for two years before ending his association with CBS in 1962. Bennett spent the next year as a producer for television station KNXT.

Harve joined ABC TV in 1963 as manager of program development and rose through the ranks over the next years ultimately to become vice-president, Programming, of that network. One of the many series he helped develop during that time was *Mod Squad*. He left ABC to produce it.

The Mod Squad began production in 1968, with Bennett handling both the production and writing chores. The series' heroes were three young adults who, thanks to police captain Adam Greer, made the transition from juvenile offenders to undercover policemen. Stars Michael Cole (as Pete Cochrane), Peggy Lipton (Julie Barnes) and Clarence Williams III (Linc Hayes) attained cult followings during the series' production, more so than did Tige Andrews (Captain Greer). After Bennett left the series, Tony Barrett took over as the series' producer. *Mod Squad* lasted until 1973, with a total of 124 episodes.

The Young Rebels, which Bennett created and wrote for, was an idea some five years before its time. It told of four young adults who, in Chester, Pennsylvania, in 1777, formed the secret "Yankee Doodle Society" to fight the British in the Revolutionary War. Actor Rick Ely portrayed Jeremy Larken (a man the townspeople thought harmless). Lou Gossett was Isak Poole (a blacksmith) and Hilarie Thompson was Elizabeth Coates, their associate. The most interesting member of the group was Henry Abington, an eccentric explosives expert and all-around scientific wizard who, as played by character actor Alex Hentleoff, bore a striking resemblance to a young Benjamin Franklin. Also on their side was the young French general, the Marquis de Lafayette (Philippe Forquet). Because of the undercover nature of their work, *The Young Rebels* emerged as a sort of period piece *Mod Squad*. The series, whose producer was Aaron Spelling, ran only thirteen episodes. Had it been produced during the U.S. Bicentennial celebration half a decade later, it might well have achieved a long, successful run.

In 1971, Bennett joined Universal Television as a writer and executive producer. During this period, he first became connected with the two series for which he is generally best known: *The Six Million Dollar Man* and *The Bionic Woman*.

Mr. Bennett was the executive producer of *The Six Million Dollar Man* from its inception until he left Universal five years later. During that time he was also the executive producer of the enormously successful pioneer mini-series *Rich Man, Poor Man* (1976). In that same year *Six Mil* begat yet another Bionic series.

The Bionic Woman debuted in 1976 with Bennett as executive producer. The show was an instant hit and, coupled with *The Six Million Dollar Man* and *Rich Man, Poor Man,* gave Bennett the heady experience of having the top three Nielsen-rated shows in America for ten consecutive weeks.

Harve left Universal in 1977 and next assumed the presidency of Bennett-Katleman Television Productions, with headquarters at Columbia Pictures studios. His partner, Harris Katleman, was a former head of MGM Television. Together the two worked at creating and developing properties for Columbia motion pictures and television.

Bennett's many accomplishments have earned him honors which include two Writers' Guild Award nominations for *Mod Squad* scripts in 1969 and 1970. He won the "Edgar" Award (named after Edgar Allan Poe, this is the mystery world's equivalent to the Oscar) for a *Mod Squad* script, and in 1976 he won the Golden Globe Award for his miniseries, *Rich Man, Poor Man* (Book I). In addition, he has garnered 26 Emmy Award nominations (including *Mod Squad,* for best series in 1969 and 1970, and *Rich Man, Poor Man* (Book One) as 1976's best miniseries.

Returning to pleasant, nostalgic memories, Bennett attempted to revive the *Quiz Kids* series in 1980. Episodes were produced with Norman Lear acting as the series host; the series is no longer in production.

While associated with Universal, Harve Bennett experienced an incident that made him wary of series' more ardent "fans." In March, 1977, he received a telephone call from a man identifying himself as the President's Press Secretary, Jody Powell. He said young Amy Carter was a great fan of Lee Majors and, if the producer could furnish the actor's home telephone number, Amy would invite Majors to her birthday party. Bennett gave the caller the phone number, but later learned Powell had never actually called; he'd been hoaxed! When the bogus caller struck again, the irate producer told him, "You're not the real Jody Powell," and the unknown trickster hung up.

One of Bennett's other series projects was *The Invisible Man,* which starred David MacCallum as a scientist who had rendered himself transparent and was therefore in great demand by the U.S. government, foreign powers and underworld figures. Unfortunately, the series was not in as great demand as its hero; it was cancelled after only eleven episodes had been produced.

In a 1976 magazine article pertaining to *The Invisible Man,* Bennett observed that "There are certain patterns in an adventure series that you vary at your peril," and admitted " . . . Frankly, we varied quite a few, and we paid the price." Perhaps this realization explains the vehemence with which Bennett set out to preserve the original parameters of the *Star Trek* format.

Harve Bennett, who was married in 1962 and is now divorced, has two children: Christopher Emil Bennett, born in 1968, and Susan Amanda Bennett, born in 1970.

The executive producer's interests include flying, skiing and playing tennis. He has also owned his own airplane and show horses.

His interests have now broadened out to a literally cosmic scale since his introduction to the world of *Star Trek.*

Harve Bennett's Television Credits

A Woman Called Golda (Syndicated miniseries, 1982, Executive Producer)

American Girls (CBS miniseries, 1978, Executive Producer with Harris Katleman)

Bionic Woman, The (ABC: 1975–78, NBC: 1977–78, Executive Producer)

Frankie Laine Time (CBS, 1955–56, Associate Producer)

From Here to Eternity (NBC miniseries, 1979, Executive Producer)

Gemini Man, The (NBC, 1977, Executive Producer)

Invisible Man, The (NBC, 1976, Executive Producer)

Johnny Carson Show, The (CBS, 1954, Associate Producer)

Mod Squad (ABC, 1968–71, Developer, Writer, Producer)

Powers of Matthew Starr, The (NBC, debuted 1982, Executive Producer)

Red Skelton Show, The (CBS, debuted 1953, Associate Producer)

Rich Man, Poor Man: Book I (ABC miniseries, 1976, Executive Producer)

Robert Q. Lewis Show, The (CBS, 1964–65, Associate Producer)
Salvage I (ABC, 1978–79, Executive Producer)
Sam Shepard Murder Case, The (Television Movie, 1976, Executive Producer)
Six Million Dollar Man, The (ABC, 1974–78, Executive Producer)
Young Rebels, The (ABC, 1970–71, Creator and Scriptwriter)

   Upon meeting Harve Bennett, one becomes aware that this man possesses an extraordinary ability to communicate. Coupled with his interests in history and storytelling, this talent accounts for his high degree of success as the one single individual most responsible for *Star Trek II: The Wrath of Khan*.

   Mr. Bennett also has the gift of enabling an interviewer to feel completely comfortable in his presence. Undoubtedly, this gift also holds true regarding the personnel involved with Bennett on his projects. Every individual I spoke to about *Star Trek II* invariably mentioned that it was very enjoyable to work on the film and that they always felt comfortable talking about their role in the movie.

QUESTION—*Where do most of your creative inspirations come from?*

HB — The body of my work has been literally adaptive. Most of the things that I have successfully done well have not been my own creations but adaptations of other people's original material. *Mod Squad*, of course, was someone else's idea that I fleshed out with Aaron [Spelling]. The "bionics" shows were both based on Martin Caiden's novel. *Rich Man, Poor Man* was an Irwin Shaw novel, which I adapted with the hand of Dean Reisner writing it, and so on. Adaptation is a medium with which I feel very comfortable. . . . Actually, if I have a credo about whatever it is I do, it comes from the man who I admire to this day most in my field, David Lean. David Lean once spoke at the Directors' Guild. . . . He made a very short speech, of which the most memorable phrase was, "People ask me what, if any, contribution I have made to film, and I only have one answer, and that is the reason why I have done all this, and hope to continue to do it: I am a storyteller. I like a good yarn." And he sat down. I thought that was the most succinct expression of what it is about what I do that I like. I like a good yarn.

Q — *But you also have to have the wisdom to look at a good property and sense its dramatique to adapt it.*

HB — I'd be the last person to argue with that statement. On the other hand, we're talking about this at a very peculiar time in the evolution of film, or whatever it is in this year, in this decade. There is an enormous amount of current conversation and written material about this art form, and I'm always amused by that because I'm sure that there were wonderful discussions in the sixteenth century about . . . styles, and what makes art fine, because everybody likes to talk about it. Fine. At the very base of what I believe about material is a very simple feeling. It's hard to intellectualize, and I hate it when I try. I do like a good yarn, and I know what *makes* a good yarn, but I can't *tell you* what makes a good yarn. I can't intellectualize it, because the minute I start to, I fall into the very trap which is anti-art: trying to make scientific that which is not.

Q — *If there was, I'm sure somebody would have a formula to figure it out.*

HB — Yes. A computer would therefore theoretically tell a story; and the answer is that it can't. If there is a rule, however . . . the rule is that a good yarn requires that you root for somebody, that you care about somebody enough to be sucked out of yourself into the art, into the experience. Otherwise you always remain outside the experience as an observer rather than as an emotional participant. And that's about as far as I care to go intellectually to describe what a good story is.

Q — *Did you feel this quality in the* Star Trek *television series?*

HB — Episode after episode . . . I was always rooting for somebody. The essence of the series was allegory developed into
highly intense personal conflict. Grand opera in a lot of
ways. And here was the perfect cast to do that kind of
specific style. Each actor's personal style became fused
into this operatic style; very uncommon to the screen.
When Nick [Meyer] was a professor in Iowa, he used to say
that *Star Trek* was a radio play. . . . He used to have an
exercise in which a class was asked to watch *Star Trek,* then
watch *Mission: Impossible,* I believe. Then he would ask
them to listen to one without the picture, and the next week
the other, and the results were obvious. *Star Trek* could be
listened to and understood. If you deprived *Mission: Impossible* of the picture, you were lost. You couldn't tell
from the sound what the story was. *Star Trek* could be
discerned from the sound alone; that is to say, the classic
radio play. I think that was very true.

Q — *Right down to the Captain's Log device.*

HB — Yes. And all the devices of storytelling in the series itself
were radio devices, and for a lot of good reasons. There's
no way, under the budgetary restrictions of a series, to do
as much as the imaginative people doing it would have liked
to have done.

Q — *Did you like* all *the* Star Trek *episodes?*

HB — I'm not saying that all the episodes work by far; no series
has that kind of track record, but I think a third of the *Star
Trek* episodes were extraordinarily good, and that's really
an amazing series . . . and another third were illuminated
by the fact that the characters and the themes, and everything else, always had something interesting to deal with.

Q — *What were your first thoughts after you were asked by
Paramount to work on Star Trek II?*

HB — My first gut reaction was negative, because I didn't want to do somebody else's legend. I had just come to Paramount. I had a track record of some size, and what appealed to me was its potential as my first feature picture. For some reason or another, I had never done a feature picture. . . . I really went right past the fact that I would really have to do an enormous amount of homework, from my own standards, not for anybody else's, in order to truly digest and be respectful to the material. This is a compulsion that's mine. A lot of people could come in and do a "tap dance." One of my great strengths—and I suppose weaknesses—is that I don't like to do lip service to something that has worth. And the one thing I was certain about was that, clearly, this had worth. *Star Trek* is a phenomenon, is a project . . . and if nothing else is an avenue of expression in a medium that was getting drier and drier and drier . . . I think it is not illogical that *Star Trek* reruns, during the 1970s, fulfilled a need that network television was not fulfilling. My own network television days during that time were successful enough, but I can't tell you that *The Six Million Dollar Man* fulfilled a deep, philosophical satisfaction for me. It was a job well done, it was a yarn well told; I would never think of doing a feature picture about *The Six Million Dollar Man*. That I would turn down.

Q — *After you made up your mind to go ahead, how difficult was it to accomplish?*

HB — I'd describe this entire eighteen months as a series of minefields. Nothing was easy. It seems easy now. There wasn't a single achievement, decision, step forward that wasn't a problem. I don't mean to glamourize my role as the person who started with "Okay, I'll do it," and ended up with the picture . . . but in point of fact, I don't know how I did it. . . . Everything that had to go right went right. And I can think of a hundred places where I would have happily said, "It's no use . . . we can't."

Q — *What sort of assistance did you get?*

HB — DeForest Kelley pointed something out to me that I already understood intellectually: the core of *Star Trek* is a triangular relationship with Kirk at the top and Bones and Spock at the corners. Every critic of *Star Trek* has sooner or later come to that isosceles triangle. It is correct. And he felt that the first script did not reflect that, that [McCoy] was being used at random. Now, in what other major feature picture in the world would an actor turn down an opportunity to be seen by potentially forty million people because he wasn't being used in the proper relationship to a triangle? Only in *Star Trek.* And in point of fact, the final result of his comment, along with many other factors, I think made a better picture. I have never been one who felt that the input of everybody wasn't part of the process. The making of a movie is not an "auteur" situation, notwithstanding all the auteurs in our business. And I think that Nick [Meyer], who is as close to an auteur as I have known, would be the first to agree with that. It is a combination of skills, and it has always been my job, whether for television or for this big screen, to keep the team working together, to cross the minefields, to compromise when necessary, and to say yes and no. . . . This project was the maximum and ultimate test of my ability to do that. . . .

Q — *Anyone else give you assistance?*

HB — Karen Moore was the head of development at Paramount when I came. She's one of those people who's a catalytic friend to everybody. She's a behind-the-scenes earth mother who makes people patch up their differences and gets things done when all looks hopeless. I don't think we would have made this picture without Karen. It was Karen who kept me from going crazy. It was also Karen who first took me to see Leonard [Nimoy].

Q — *How did Leonard Nimoy and William Shatner first react upon being approached to do Star Trek II?*

HB — I showed the first outline, "The War of the Generations," to Bill Shatner. Bill and I knew each other; he had done a *Six Million Dollar Man* episode, probably the best I ever did ("Burning Bright"). We had grown to respect each other. He knew what I could do, and I certainly knew what he could do. . . . One thing was certain to me . . . that no *Star Trek* would be interesting unless he [Captain Kirk] was in charge. . . . Bill perceived that I saw that, so getting Bill aboard was relatively easy.

Q — *. . . And Leonard Nimoy?*

HB — I had worked with Leonard once or twice. He did a [TV] movie for me at Universal called *The Alpha Caper*. It was delightful, and we liked each other a lot. . . . Of all the *Star Trek* actors, he's the one who's . . . the most bemused by the afterlife of the show; by the lines, and by the activity and by the adulation. It embarrasses him, and that's irony because the misperception of him out there is that Leonard is the most cantankerous and ego-driven. Quite the contrary; he's the guy who doesn't want it. For such a man to be a character who's so specific—he did such a good job, and Gene's concept and everybody's work was so specific that of all the actors in the world . . . he was the most defined. I'll tell you one story that will be the definition of what I'm trying to say. I told my son Christopher Bennett, "I've got to go see Leonard Nimoy, Chris . . . would you like to come?" "Oh, sure." And then instantly, without anyone having to tell me, I said to my son, "Oh, by the way Chris, try not to stare at his ears." I stopped myself, and in so saying, I understood the Nimoy dilemma. And sure enough, Christopher said hello, and he couldn't avoid . . . And Leonard noticed and we laughed about it, and I said "I understand." . . . Of all the creations of television, there is no question that Mr. Spock will live for a very long time. . . . Leonard has coped with it and gone on to vigorous intellectual activity . . . and as I'm sure you know, he wrote a series of essays entitled "I Am Not Spock." Okay. I'm as

good a salesman as the next person, but I never like to
convince someone to do something they don't want to do.
. . . I was perfectly willing to accept the fact that getting
Leonard into this movie was going to be an impossible task.
I did leave it open. . . . I said, "If I come up with a story
that appeals to you, is the door still open?" And he said,
"Of course."

Q — *Did he at any time ask you to kill Spock?*

HB — No. Never. We started to work, and after many, many
considerations, I chose Jack Sowards, and Jack made an
enormous contribution to this picture. . . . Jack and I went
to work, and I say *we* went to work because the process is
like this: you talk, and you rap, and the responsibility is that
the writer records, in whatever fashion he chooses . . . the
fruits of the give and take of this process. His task is then to
go and make it become a script. In the course of those
discussions, he said, "It would be a shame to do it without
Leonard," and I said, "I know, but, umm . . ." He said,
"Why don't we kill [Spock]?" . . . And I said, "I think
that's great. I bet you I can convince Leonard that that's
the reason to come back one more time." I went to see
Leonard. . . . I said, "Leonard, I think I know how to get
you into *Star Trek*." And he said, "Go ahead . . ." I said,
"Leonard, remember *Psycho,* and did you see *Dressed to
Kill?*" He said yeah, and his smile got bigger and bigger. I
said, "Well, that's what we're going to do with Mr. Spock."
And he said, "That's fantastic!" And right then and there
we shook hands and that was it. Now, that was the
beginning of an evolution that got so convoluted that its
resemblance to the final film is, of course, a process.

Q — *Is that why Spock was killed off so early in the first drafts?*

HB — Sure . . . The course is now easy for me to plot . . . [it] was
simple. I persuaded Leonard to do it because it was going to
be theatrical, and the theatricality rested on shock . . . on
surprise. We therefore drafted that it happened in the first

third of the script. The studio thought that was wonderful. In addition to that, I offered Leonard an opportunity to play Morris Meyerson in *Golda* to prove our faith in him as an actor. . . . I'm going to jump to the next significant event in the evolution of this particular part of the project. With the first draft script in and available only to the inner circle of people working on *Star Trek,* an individual who had been sent her own personal script and who was pledged to secrecy went to a *Star Trek* convention in London, England, and publicly announced the death of Spock—not only announced it but blamed it on Paramount Pictures. "They're killing Spock," she said. And this after she had personally promised me that no details of the script would be made public. Well, not only had the whole theatricality of our surprise been compromised, but this betrayal hit every newspaper in the world, beginning with the *Wall Street Journal.* The impact was staggering. Everyone from the studio to Leonard Nimoy was inflamed. The studio now said, "You can't kill Spock," and Leonard, who received everything from hate mail to threats on his family's lives, was seriously and justifiably thinking of backing out. "I did not sign on to be accused of murder," he correctly observed. We began to deal positively, however, with these events. It changed our thinking on the script because, clearly, if Spock was to die, his death would now have to be the climax of the picture. Surprise was out of the question. In addition we would have to defuse the lunatic fringe of *Star Trek* fans who were whipping up hate mail and doing self-serving things like taking personal polls to get their names in the paper over this hot news controversy. Out of this need, I created a policy which I called "Throwing Tinfoil into the Radar Sets." This policy resulted in endless conflicting statements about the death of Spock. None were lies, but all were half-truths. The purpose of the policy was clear, and it worked. It could not restore surprise; so instead it established ambiguity. This was the purpose of the alternate-ending rumors. The philosophy worked. The anger was diffused and people saw the film with an uncertainty that at least restored the freshness of our film. Perhaps in the long view I should hug the lady who betrayed us, rather than be angry, since the turmoil of all these events resulted in a much better picture.

Q — *Where did the title* Star Trek: The Undiscovered Country *come from?*

HB — That was Nicholas Meyer's title. It's from *Hamlet,* from Hamlet's soliloquy. It's death, ". . . The undiscovered country, from whose bourn / No traveller returns . . ."

Q — *Everything ties together.*

HB — Well, it not only ties together, but from my sense of unity it was as Stephen Leacock once wrote: ". . . galloping off in all directions." It was filled with classical allusions.

Q — *The structure of* Star Trek II, *in some respects, is very reminiscent of a classic Laurel and Hardy comedy routine.*

HB — I once read a book years ago, by Karel Reisz, editor and director. He chose Laurel and Hardy, too, for a different reason. He said the essence of all film editing is illustrated by the following scene, and he chose this classic scene: You are given three shots. Long shot: Laurel and Hardy walk down the street. Close shot: banana peel. Long shot: a continuation of the first shot. Hardy slips. He then proceeds to make the case that where you place the close shot is of the essence, because if you have them walking down the street and continue the shot, and Hardy falls, then you cut to the banana peel, it is explanatory, and in the process you've created what he now calls "surprise." The reverse: walking down the street, cut to the banana peel, slip on the banana peel, is called "anticipation," or suspense. He now says that all editorial choices are either surprise or suspense. Well, my fertile mind said from this, "Well, what do you mean, editorial choices?" Storytelling choices stem from this choice, which I firmly believe in to this day. Nicholas [Meyer] understands that. If he wasn't guided by it specifically as I was, the moment I told him the story he said, "Of course." At all times, in this tale, as it reworked itself, I was always mindful of suspense versus surprise. And the achievement of the film, structurally, is that just when you think you're in a suspense situation, you get surprised. . . . Any other similarity, as you pointed out, is probably indigenous to the process: that all good comedy is the juxtaposition of character attitudes, which engender suspense or surprise.

Q — *Was there an attempt to show that Spock was aware of his impending death, as was Queequeg in* Moby Dick?

HB — I argued vigorously with Nick that the precognition exhibited by Spock was inappropriate. Spock is not a mystic; he does not know he's going to die, and the fact that he chose *A Tale of Two Cities* indicated that Nick was trying to do something theatrical rather than legitimate. He said, "But it works." I would say that fifty percent of the time I would give in to Nick, and fifty percent of the time I wouldn't. This didn't matter to me . . . we did it that way. Naturally, the perception of the whole when you see the picture does not include the rivulets of disagreement between seventeen people for how it should be. The assumption is that one intelligence guided it, which is not true.

Q — *That's the magic of movies, isn't it?*

HB — That's right. The extent that all the decisions tended to be uniform in nature. We were all on the same course, and we loved each other. The issue of Spock's precognition was thus a difference of interpretation. I would have excised it—but I went with Nick's intuition. . . . These are the kinds of things that you get into, the questions of taste and judgment, which is the living process called making a movie.

Q — *I understand you and Meyer had some disagreements and difficulties over the simulator scene.*

HB — Yes, but we came to each other's aid ultimately. . . . I was in London doing *Golda* for the first five days of the *Star Trek II* shoot, and that was almost disastrous. We shot pretty much in continuity, and the simulator scene was done first. . . . It was his first day's shoot, and it was criminal to throw any director into the most difficult scene because you're starting a picture cold after two years of waiting for *Star Trek,* and everything is hanging on a trick. If the trick is too real, and then you say, "It's just a trick, folks," the audience will be furious. If the trick is too shabby, you've lost the audience in the first five minutes of the picture, and you may never recover them. After the endless discussions as to what the simulator sequence was to be, he got too real with it. There were people flying through the air. We were concerned that we were going to get laughs when we revealed it was a simulation. It was the only major reshoot we did. . . . My mistake was that I had Kirk on the bridge standing around. Nick wanted to place Kirk outside the simulator room, seated in a corridor, reading *A Tale of Two Cities.* Bob Sallin and I argued that doing so would interrupt the dramatic build of that scene, and suggested that Kirk emerge, in true Wagnerian fashion, from behind the sliding viewscreen wall, engulfed in smoke and strongly backlit. And, of course, that is precisely what we did. The entrance became one of those theatrical moments that you remember in the film. The other thing Nick said, which is why the collaboration was so wonderful . . . after all that we went through regarding the death of Spock, we're now three days into shooting, we're on the bridge, people are dropping like flies, and Nicholas says, "We've got to kill Spock." And I said, "That's fantastic," whereupon I said that in scene three, when Kirk comes out, and Spock's waiting for him, I want Kirk to say, "Aren't you dead?" Nick said why, it would be gilding the lily, and I said no, no . . . it would convince the audience that Spock's death has already happened. I hope . . . that I am blessed with Nick, or with anyone, with so vivid a collaboration. It was like saying, "You thought we fooled you about Spock's

death? You're right, we fooled you. So just sit back and
watch the picture. Then we'll fool you again." Nick perceived the reasoning and went with my instinct, and it
worked. . . . I hope that I am blessed with Nick again, or
with anyone who can create so vivid a collaboration. That
was the nature and the joy of the making of this picture, and
it went on down through the very end of the film. It never
stopped being a living thing.

Q — *The entire theme of the Kobayashi Maru scenario is so
intriguing. Can you mention anything regarding the evolution of the "running joke" regarding Kirk's handling of it?*

HB — Nicholas Meyer mined that much more heavily than I did.
All the subsequent use of that concept was pure Meyer:

"He's dead, Jim?" DeForest Kelley, Kirstie Alley, and Merritt Butrick
enjoy De's birthday party

Nicholas extracting the essence of something we had stumbled upon as the thematic essence of the picture. For example, traditionalist me and iconoclast Meyer quarreled over Kirk changing the conditions of the test.

Q — *It's something Kirk would do.*

HB — But I missed that in my reverence for *Star Trek*. I said, "You can't have him cheating," and Nick looked at me and said the cruelest words he ever said: "Television Mentality." Twenty-five years of having broadcast standards pound you with *McGuffey Reader* reasons for doing things, you get inured to it, and you suddenly find yourself doing things because they are more morally acceptable to the majority. And it was quite an experience for me, having someone say to me, "Why can't Kirk cheat," to which I had no answer at all, except to ask whether it was in his character, and the answer you've just expressed—yes. Of course it is.

Q — *Considering the pressures your production was under, would you say there were generally good feelings on the set?*

HB — I would say that, as a generality, the . . . cast essentially had a fabulous time. No matter how great or small their parts were, because of many factors there was great joy on that set. I think Nicholas was an enormous joyful force, that Leonard was happy . . . there was dissension on the set, and there were always creative arguments, but there was none of the nonsense that all of us who make pictures have seen from time to time, where people don't talk to people, people don't go on the stage until someone else appears . . . there was none of that nonsense. It was a happy set.

Q — *What about the rumors of alternate endings? Was there any truth to them?*

HB — We never changed the ending of the picture. But we changed reel twelve. There is a very interesting difference in that. The ending of the picture was that Spock dies. We never changed that. That was never a question or an issue with us. . . . What we changed was the texture of the perception of that death. And to prove how complicated an argument that was, it is true that we made it many things to many people. It's interesting being out on the street now and finding out who believes what. The fact of the matter is that those who are inclined to be pragmatic will take one view, those who are philosophical will take another and those who are absolutely childlike will take the third. It is, like a good magician's trick, however, possible to puncture everybody's perception of the ending by asking one question: "What do you think is in the casket?" And the answer is *I* don't know what's in there; I have no validation that there is anything in there at all. The fact of the matter is that it became a metaphysical ending instead of "Goodbye." We commissioned that shot, and Bob Sallin went to San Francisco, to of all places Golden Gate Park, which is ironic because the picture begins in San Francisco. When it came back, I don't think any of us could have told you that we were going to support it. I made the decision after I first saw it on the screen, but I asked Nick to wait until James [Horner] had done the score. We tracked it with a Spock theme which James had already recorded. But we had one more day of recording, and I showed it to Nick for the first time on the dubbing stage. The ultimate reason why we all agreed to use it was simple . . . it gives us something that we did not have. It is a beautiful ending to a beautiful film.

Robert S. Sallin

Robert Sallin graduated the University of California, Los Angeles (UCLA) after attending that institution of higher learning from 1949–1953. A distinguished Air Force ROTC graduate, he also won the Southern Campus Honor Award and the Bronze Theater Award. Sallin earned his B.A. degree in film production.

While in the United States Air Force, from 1954–58, he was a motion picture officer, functioning as a director, producer and writer of documentaries and coverage of Air Force activities throughout various areas of the world. During this period, he worked at film production in some of the most uncomfortable places on earth, as well as less stringent locales such as Paris, France.

Making use of his valuable Air Force experience, Sallin became the assistant to the producer on the NBC television series *Steve Canyon*. It was his responsibility to attend to preproduction planning. He also arranged the securing of Air Force aircraft (including B-52s and F-104s), as well as directing scenes shot on location for integration into the finished episodes.

Switching to the hectic world of television commercial production, Robert then joined the Los Angeles staff of the Foote, Cone and Belding Advertising Agency, where he was a company vice-president. In this capacity of director of TV commercial production for their Western offices, he was responsible for the genesis of commercials for some of the biggest national accounts of the agency, a job of constant pressure-filled production tasks.

Robert Sallin, producer of *Star Trek II: The Wrath of Khan*

After almost seven years of the most demanding tasks in this area, he quit the company in 1966 to form his own company, Kaleidoscope Productions.

Sallin's successful venture led him to direct and produce more than 1600 national and international commercials, working for some of the world's largest businesses and directing some of the most famous models and entertainers in the world.

The recipient of top awards in the commercial field, Sallin's impressive list of honors includes the 1978 Clio Award (for the Most Humorous Commercial of the Year) and the 1970 Grand Prix for the outstanding commercial of the world (awarded at the Venice Film Festival).

His directorial experience includes episodes of the television series *Sunshine*, the *First Bill Cosby Special* (the opening segment) and an episode of *American Girls* (produced by Harve Bennett).

Sallin first met Harve Bennett while they were both attending UCLA. Both men were aware of each other's abilities and track records in addition to having a working relationship. When Bennett first realized the enormous complexity involved in mounting *Star Trek II,* he concluded that Sallin, with his knowledge of complex film techniques, business acumen, and success as a director, would be the logical choice for making sure that the complete production could come together as smoothly and as quickly as possible.

Sallin is a man who will always appear to be much younger than his true age due to an ever-present elation about his work. This is a quality he shares with Bennett and, when coupled with the energy of Nicholas Meyer, is the characteristic that breathed life into *Star Trek II*.

QUESTION—*Can you think of any specific instances of holding the production costs down in* Star Trek II?

RS — One small incident comes to mind, more because of its amusing aspect than anything else. Nick Meyer asked for what I considered a really interesting shot in the torpedo bay. He wanted to drop the camera down into the trough and truck along with the photon torpedo. . . . Unfortunately, the set had been designed without that in mind, because he [Nick] hadn't thought of it at the time. The set, in order to save money, utilized parts of the Klingon bridge from the previous movie. . . . The production people came to me and said [the modifications] would have to be done over the weekend and at nights, and "it's going to cost between five and ten thousand dollars because we have to tear out the whole trough to restructure it and accommodate the weight, and brace it. . . ." And I said, "Hold it, a meeting on that stage in ten minutes." So I assembled everybody and I looked at it, and I asked if we could get our hands on some dolly track, the round stuff. "Yeah." Okay . . . put it down on top of the trough, and make it look like it's a part of the set and anchor it. "Oh, yeah, we can do that." Great. I said, get a "Western dolly," make a larger set of axles, take off the balloon tires and put on the wheels that go with the tubular track. Can we do that? "Yeah." I said, we can drop the camera right down there, can't we? They said, "Yes." I said, terrific. How much will it cost? And they looked at me and said, "About twenty-nine dollars." And that's exactly what we did.

Q — *Is it true that you left room, beneath the casket in the pickup shot on the planet, to superimpose "New and Improved," as if you were shooting a commercial?*

RS — [Laughter] That's what I told everybody. Because of my commercial production background, I couldn't help but view the casket shot as being very similar in style to hundreds of "product" shots which I had directed. I broke up when I was doing it, because as we craned over and up to disclose the casket, I kept thinking there was a lot of room for the two-line super. And I thought afterwards, because it is very often what is done with product shots, "I wonder if we shouldn't shoot another version with NEW on it." One version with NEW is used in commercials for the first six months, and then the title is removed. . . . In terms of visual style, as any filmmaker does, one draws upon those techniques which are applicable to solve a problem. We wanted to be mystical but happy, uplifting and not morose. And that's why we had the mixture of sunlight and pumped-in smoke.

Q   — *The music carries that across, too.*

RS — Oh, absolutely. Our composer, James Horner, was very much my first choice. I listened to an enormous number of cassettes. . . . In listening to them, I was bored by what passes for musical wallpaper. It doesn't go anywhere, and it doesn't evoke anything. It fills space. It's a background music, such as one hears in an elevator. And as I listened to other composers' work I was impressed with the work of this young man, James Horner. And again, I wanted someone who was eager, someone who wasn't well established, someone who would kill to get this opportunity. And literally, James gave his all. And all of us were thrilled and delighted. What I got was in some ways a traditional score, but certainly a melodic score, which was very appropriate for our kind of picture. What we have here is a space opera, and I think the music works well with it. James is twenty-eight years old. But he got up there and handled that ninety-piece orchestra like the pro he is.

Q   — *It must be a very inspiring thing to see.*

RS — It's one of my very favorite parts of production. I had only been involved with one other feature; I replaced the director on a picture called *Picasso Summer* some years ago. My score was done by Michel Legrand. I went to Paris and scored for six days with the bulk of the Paris Conservatory Orchestra. It was a thrill. I love music . . . and also, to be perfectly honest, when those opening credits come up, and your name is there, and ninety pieces are going full out, it makes you feel very good.

Q   — *How did the previews for this movie go?*

RS — They were really wonderful. I think that one of the high points in the whole experience was not only the previews we held here at the studio, but certainly the one in Kansas City. . . . If, as a producer, I sat down to write a script about how I wanted a preview to go, I couldn't have topped what really happened.

Q — *Did you know anything about* Star Trek *when you joined this production?*

RS — Not in any great detail. Of course, I watched episodes over the years when it first came out, and . . . as a matter of fact, I had once used Nichelle Nichols in a commercial that I directed many, many years ago . . . I believe it was for Procter & Gamble. But again, in answer to your question, I had watched an occasional episode and was not really committed as a fan. And I think that helped, in many ways. . . . I always felt, as Harve did, that we had to pay homage to the tradition—but not to become enslaved by it. And I think that enabled both Harve and myself . . . because he was not a fan, either . . . to approach the story, and how we did things and what we did with them, with a little more freedom and freshness.

Q — *How did the young Genesis scientists enter the picture?*

RS — Originally, Harve's thought on that was that it should be a futuristic version of Kent State. And in one draft, the young scientists were on a planet, and they went into an amphitheater where there was a shoot-out between them and Terrell and Chekov. David, as a character, was in fact to be what he is . . . a young scientist, head of that group of young people, not rebels but doubters.

Q — *Was there any reason why some of the recurring characters' roles were not larger?*

RS — How do you tell the kind of story that you have to tell in under two hours and give everybody emphasis? Something has to give. It's not that we didn't want to make everyone's parts larger, but candidly the realities were such that you just couldn't do that. We couldn't accommodate anymore and tell an intelligible tale. We had David, Saavik, Khan and his followers, Terrell; we've got all those people. It could have become *War and Peace*.

Q — *Are you planning on doing* Star Trek III?

RS — I have mixed feelings about that. Number one, I am a director. I have made my living directing since I was fifteen years old, when I used to direct for NBC radio. I've done it most of my life. If they asked me to direct it, I would be very receptive to that. If I'm asked to produce again, my feeling at this time is no. I don't know what there is for me to be gained professionally by producing it a second time. It's not that I don't love the people. It was really a joy to work with everyone on this show. But I don't see that producing *Star Trek III* does anything to take me where I want to go, which is back to directing.

Q — *Had you done any reading in science fiction before you did this project?*

RS — Not with any great emphasis. Over the years, I had read Ray Bradbury, Heinlein, Asimov and some others, but not with any dedication. It was merely part of the general reading pattern I had, which was to read anything that struck me as potentially being a good yarn.

Q — *It appears that you treated this movie more or less like a period piece.*

RS — I hadn't thought of it like that. Yes, or another creative problem to be solved. How do you attack that, and how do you give it a fresh vision? How do you build on that . . . which was already good . . . and hopefully make it better? And make it fresher? This is one of the reasons why I had written a memo to Harve, even before Nick joined the

project, saying that one of the first things we had to do was
redesign the entire wardrobe. I knew we couldn't afford to
do *all* the wardrobe over again, and 'way back I had gotten
Bob Fletcher to run some dye tests to find out what colors
the old uniforms from *Star Trek: The Motion Picture* would
take successfully. We ended up with three colors: a gold, a
blue-gray and the wine that we ultimately ended up with.
And Bob Fletcher, who is a wonderful talent, added things,
and we changed things, including the tightness of the fit. He
said, "Yes . . . I can loosen this, drop that . . ." I suggested
blousing the trousers and adding the stripes. In so doing, we
were able to modify and reuse much of the previous
wardrobe for the cadets' uniforms. Now, that's not true, of
course, for the officers' uniforms. The cadet officers, and
the others, were all done from scratch. And that arose out
of Nick's idea. His phrase was . . . "The Prisoner of
Zenda." And I thought that was a neat idea. The original
designs for those were almost the way they are, with three
major exceptions. It had a stiff black collar, and I said it's
going to look like West Point or a page at the Beverly Hills
Hotel. So, I suggested we drop the collar, do a round neck,
and use turtlenecks. And then Bob Fletcher said, "We'll
make it quilted." . . . Trapunto, which is a form of vertical
quilting. I said, let's make it in all the colors of the original
divisions. And Bob said, "A great idea. I'll add it to the
shoulder strap, too." Then I thought it might be visually dull
throughout the whole picture, to see everybody zipped up
like that. We redesigned it so the lapels or flaps could open.
I then suggested facing them with a light color, because it
would help frame the faces better and it would give a little
"snap" to the design. Finally, there was one minor adjustment: the small band that's now positioned low on the
sleeve was originally up higher, not unlike a World War Two
German uniform. I thought that was a potentially negative
element, hence the repositioning.

Q — *How did you react to the mail coming in regarding the death of Spock?*

RS — We knew that people would be upset . . . we knew that people cared. I think that perhaps to a certain extent we were a little surprised by the intensity of the feeling. . . . I admired the fact that they cared, but in terms of whether or not it influenced us, the answer is not a lot. We felt that this was going to be an honest movie, and that you don't pussyfoot around with this type of story. I'm not telling you there wasn't any concern, because there was an enormous amount, but we shot the picture the way we set out to shoot it. And the only difference in the ending, because there was some discussion as to whether or not there were alternate endings, is that we *did* add that sequence that I shot up at Golden Gate Park. And that was Harve's idea. It was his idea to do it, and it was my idea as to what the shots should be and where they should be filmed. I think the idea of doing that sequence on the planet was a sound one, because it gave the audience a moment to recover. It's only sixty seconds long; in fact, I laughed when we edited the sequence. I said, I can't seem to break away from the sixty-second commercial format. But it just seemed to work out well at that length.

Q — *Did you ever want to shoot the casket open?*

RS — No, I didn't.

Nicholas Meyer

Nicholas Meyer was born in New York City in 1945.[1] He wrote and acted in his first film at thirteen, a 70-minute opus filmed in 8mm whose production was inspired by the artist's first viewing of *Around the World in Eighty Days*.

Nicholas attended a private high school in Riverdale, New York, before studying literature and film at the University of Iowa. He was graduated there in 1968.

After graduation, Meyer returned to New York City, anxious to break into the film industry. Although he wrote to every major film company in New York, his first job turned out to be as a pipe salesman in a Big Apple department store called Bloomingdale's.

Meyer successfully made the transition to the film business when he joined the publicity department at Paramount Pictures in New York. After nine months, he became the unit publicist on the motion picture *Love Story* and was subsequently hired by the story department of Warner Brothers.

Meyer's first book was an account of the making of *Love Story* called *The LOVE STORY Story*," published in 1971 by Avon Books. He wrote the book in just six weeks and sold it for $3,000.

In 1971 he took the $3,000 grubstake and drove west to Hollywood, hoping to find work writing for the movies.

To occupy himself during that time, he wrote *The Seven Percent Solution,* his first bestseller. The novel, which deals with the efforts of Dr. Sigmund Freud to cure Sherlock Holmes of his addiction to cocaine, was an extremely logical project for Meyer to tackle. (His father, noted psychoanalyst/author Dr. Bernard C. Meyer, wrote *Houdini: A Mind In Chains*.)

Meyer's other books include *Target Practice*,[2] *The West End Horror*,[3] *Black Orchid*[4] and *Confessions of a Homing Pigeon*.[5]

In a 1979 interview,[6] Meyer said that he sees himself as a storyteller, and that he's always wanted to direct movies. He had directed on stage and radio and thought he was better at directing than writing, explaining, "Writing was just something I always did."[7]

While at the University of Iowa, Nicholas had met writer Karl Alexander. Optioning Alexander's novel *The Time Travelers,* (1978) Meyer wrote a screenplay based upon the work. Together with his partner, Herb Jaffe, Meyer offered the screenplay to Warner Brothers on the condition that if it was filmed, he would direct it. The movie became *Time After Time,* one of the most beautiful escapist films ever made.[8]

Time After Time's screenplay[9] was not Meyer's first; he had co-written the scripts to the enjoyable, low-budget *Invasion of the Bee Girls*[10] and two TV movies, *Judge Dee* (1974) and *The Night that Panicked America* (1975), just three years before he was nominated for an Academy Award for his screenplay of *The Seven Percent Solution*.[11]

Time After Time centers around two exceptional individuals: author/sociologist/scientist H. G. Wells, and a chess-playing pal of the author's who actually turns out to be Jack the Ripper. As the police close in on the Ripper, he escapes into the future, using an experimental time machine designed and constructed by Wells. The two ultimately confront each other in a fight-to-the-death set in the San Francisco of 1979.

Time After Time does not fall into any of the clichés that sometimes inhibit science fiction movies because Meyer was more interested in making a film about individuals than science fiction. It is successful for very much the same reason as is *Star Trek II*, which is not a work of futuristic trappings or values nearly as much as it's a timeless drama of heroes and villains.

As every one of his co-workers in *Star Trek II* observed, Nicholas Meyer is an extremely energetic individual. His projects

**Director Nicholas Meyer and Leonard Nimoy in a momentary break from
production tensions**

come alive partially because he has so much of a life force and a dedication to produce good, solid entertainment that it is difficult for others working with him not to be favorably influenced by these qualities.

QUESTION—*How were you first contacted about* Star Trek II?

NM— The project was offered to me by a woman named Karen Moore. She was not empowered to confirm the offer; she *was* the first person who broached the subject. I've known her since she was about twelve . . . she's a friend of mine, and she was at my house for dinner. She was working at Paramount Pictures at the time, and she said there were two very nice fellows making this movie, Harve Bennett and Bob Sallin, and they had a good script . . . would I be interested. Then I went in to meet Harve and Bob, and got along very well. Then they showed me the first movie and I thought, "I've got to do this, because I've got to be able to do as good as this."

Q — *You had never seen* Star Trek *before that point?*

NM— No.

Q — *Did you have any feelings about being involved with science fiction or something that was contemporary mythology?*

NM— No. There're only two kinds of art . . . good and bad. The only allegiance to the content of *Star Trek* that I felt I owed was to that which struck me as good. I felt that I owed *no* allegiance to anything that was bad, for any reason whatever. My feeling, when I was working on the picture, was to divide things up with that in mind. I didn't like the costumes from any other version, so I made new costumes. I didn't like the sets, so we reworked the sets. If I didn't like the dialogue, I reworked the dialogue. Occasionally there would be screams or muttered protests from various quarters. I had loads of letters telling me how to make the movie, and we answered every one of them, saying that art is not made by committee, by taking a vote. Someone's going to have to buck the bullet, and that's *me*. And what I was really very fortunate in, Harve Bennett and Bob Sallin really supported me right down the line, from the very earliest conversations we ever had about making this film, and my ideas about what it should be. They said, "We like that, that's good, we'll support you on that." And they stayed with me. I was very lucky, because the movie was made under very chaotic conditions in terms of its post-production schedule.

Q — *Can you think of any examples?*

NM— I said I'd really like to stretch the nautical analogy. I said it should be like Captain Horatio Hornblower in outer space. I made everyone on the set watch the movie version of Hornblower. The young midshipman who gets killed . . . he's stolen right out of that movie. And it was interesting, because when I first spoke to Bill Shatner about my idea, he said, "That's interesting; that was also Gene Roddenberry's original take on it." So far, so good. But I really wanted to pursue it. I had ship's bells, and boatswain's whistles and all that sort of stuff. And we very much stressed the idea of the ships as galleons in space. There's even that scene where they start pulling up the gratings to fire the photon torpedoes; it's followed through a lot. And the other thing I kept saying: Because I'm not very interested in science fiction but I *am* interested in stories about people, the only reason for me to make this movie is if they can be real. Why can't they do things that we do now? I hate when they say "negative" when they mean "no."

Q — *Then it was basically the same kind of challenge you tackled in* Time After Time, *to make the audience care about the people?*

NM— It's *always* the same challenge. There's only two kinds of stories: good stories and bad stories. The good stories are the ones where you care what happens, and the bad stories are those in which you don't. As far as I was concerned, I said, "They don't have to go to the bathroom, but why can't Captain Kirk read a book?" I just walked into my office and pulled out a book. It was *A Tale of Two Cities.* I had no idea of how much mileage would be derived from that. And then I got the idea that Khan, who was really from 1993 or earlier, and was a super-intellect . . . the only kind of literature that would interest him would be the world's greatest. We emphasized it a little bit, in terms of John Milton, King Lear and Ahab. But I think I also make movies primarily for people who read. It doesn't mean that only people who read can get off on them, but the more you read the more you're going to get off on the little touches of that type that are in there.

Q — *So it was your idea to put in the literary allusions?*

NM— Yes.

Q — *And you chose the specific quotes as well?*

NM— Yes.

Q — *Was there any reason why Khan never removed one glove during the entire movie?*

NM— Well, it certainly got your attention, didn't it? I must preface this with something else. You have unwittingly raised a large question, which is to what degree can the artist be equated with the answers at the back of a book of math problems? To what degree is the artist's explanation of matters definitive? I'm prepared to give you a rather prosaic explanation for this. But it really, in a way, is like a magician explaining his trick. Once you've explained it, it's really rather ordinary, isn't it? But what the explanation has the net effect of doing is cancelling out any imaginative contribution that the audience might have made as to why he never removes his glove. What I really loved about it was that you *didn't* know why his glove is never removed. I

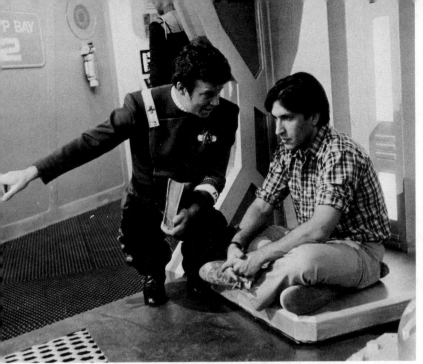

William Shatner discusses a bit of business with Nicholas Meyer

could invent a story to go with it, I could tell you how we got to it. . . . I remember when I went to a question-and-answer session with Billy Wilder at one Filmex screening. People asked the stupidest questions you ever heard people ask a director. And this is a very witty man. They asked questions . . . that you could look up in a book . . . or questions that suggested they had paid no attention to his movies. . . . The third kind of questions were the ones that troubled me the most. The kind of question that goes, "Is *One, Two, Three* a political film?" *Not* "Did you intend that it be a political film, or did it have political associations, but is it? So if he says, "Yes," and you have not had a single political association with this material, then you are "wrong," whereas if he says "No," and you have done nothing but think about the political implications in the film, then you are wrong again. In any case, *he* is being turned to as the final arbiter. The creative artist is like a man who builds a house from the inside out. The one thing he is fated never to do is to walk through the front door, go down to the end of the path, turn around and see what it is that he has done. Like Moses, he will not be allowed to cross the River Jordan. And that is why artists are always so pathetically eager for criticism, which we call "feedback." We lean out of the windows of the houses we've built and ask, "How do you like it? Are the windows big enough for you? Do you like the chimney, do you think the shutters need repainting?" And if twelve people walk by and get twelve different answers, you're doing good because then it's all personal. But if twelve people walk by and ten say that chimney is too big, then you'd better start rethinking that chimney. In other words, you look for a consensus. A lot of things in art are done by a kind of lucky accident. I don't know *why* I picked *A Tale of Two Cities*. Intuition. It was later that Shatner and Nimoy talked to me about the Charles Darnay/ Sidney Carton relationship that Kirk and Spock have. And I realized that the choice was inspired and intuitive. I can give you a mundane answer as to why he didn't take off the glove. He didn't take off the glove because he started to do it, and I said, "Don't do it . . . it looks weird that way," and I also liked the way he gestures when he says, ". . . On the *other* hand . . ." and this black claw is looking at you. It suggested something to me. It's like people said to me about *Time After Time*—who was the woman's face in the Ripper's watch? How do *I* know who she was? Who do *you* think she was? Reporters are always so startled when I say, "Why do *you* think he didn't take off the glove?" You know more than I do . . . you're the audience.

Q — *What is your impression of Harve Bennett?*

NM— I think he's great. I couldn't believe he was what he seemed to be. I kept waiting. I thought there's just too much at stake, and if I had spent as much time on this project as he has, and suddenly this whippersnapper of a kid came in and started doing this and that . . . and he went with it. He backed me to the hilt. I love that man.

Q — *And Bob Sallin was equally receptive?*

NM— Bob Sallin told me that it wasn't until they spoke to me that he ever felt (it was the day I came in and started talking about the Navy and Hornblower and whatever) that here was somebody with an overall view.

Q — *Were there many things that were determined before you joined the picture?*

NM— A lot of things were in place when I came on—the editor, the costume designer, etcetera. And the sets to the degree that they were standing sets. I said I wanted new costumes, and let's talk, and Bob Fletcher and I talked about World War I German submarine uniforms, and I said look at the uniforms of the crew of the Nautilus, and then I said what about one of these things, and they went with all those things. Bob Sallin was wonderful, because he's a man who's very long in the taste department. And because he has this enormous area of expertise from commercials, which in a way are more perfection-minded and demanding than movies, he's got this incredible eye, from which I learned a lot. I would have an overall thing about let's do something like this, but I wasn't really that experienced at judging wardrobe, and Bob would come in and talk to Bob Fletcher, and he would say things, and I'd say, "Yeah, that's right, that's good . . . " I got tremendous support from those guys. And the cast was wonderful in the same way. Nobody ever pulled rank on me.

Q — *What else did you change?*

NM— I put a lot of blinking lights around everywhere. The first day I walked around on the bridge, I was later told that in one walk I'd spent about sixty thousand dollars, just saying change this and this and this and that. Like the *No Smoking* sign. Everybody had a fit about that. "How can you do that, it's the future." And I said, why have they stopped smoking in the future? They've been smoking for four hundred years. You think it's going to stop in the next two?

Q — *What about Kirk's broken glasses at the end of the film?*

NM— What did *you* think? That's normally the way in which I answer that question. There was never a sequence in which his glasses broke. He just pulls them out of his pocket at the end, and they're broken. Something he's gone through has done it to him. Wells's glasses break, too, in *Time After Time,* during the time travel trip.

Q — *Did you ever want to get Miklos Rozsa to write the score for* Star Trek II? *One of the most wonderful facets of* Time After Time *was his score.*

NM— I thought about it, but we couldn't afford it. And I think we were lucky. I have this feeling that art thrives on restrictions, and that because we didn't have forty-two million dollars to play with, we got much more clever with creative problems. It's like the teacher says in the classroom: "Let's not always see the same hands." Why can't we see someone else? I think James Horner really did a heads-up job. He wanted it. And when I said, "Give me a nautical score . . . a rolling, sealike score," I made him a whole tape of sea music starting with Debussy's "La Mer" and Benjamin Britten's music.

Q — *Is there any last thing you want to say to the readers of this book?*

NM— My most important comment is the danger of going to the artist for definitive answers. A work of art is what the viewer makes of it. A book like this might satisfy one's curiosity about process. I would like to say that it was a lot of fun to make this movie. I loved all the people that I worked with, and I think that that love is evident on the screen; we were having a good time.

Nicholas Meyer demonstrates lifting Walter Koenig (Chekov) as Paul Winfield (Captain Terrell) looks on

Q   — *Because of your interests, which combine art and psychology, you have a unique outlook on filmmaking, don't you?*

NM— Good art bears some relationship to psychology. The greatest works of art, whether it's *King Lear,* or the "Mona Lisa" or *Oedipus,* are where art and psychology are linked and linked so effortlessly that you take it for granted. But people don't ask the questions. You have to sit there and think, "Why is this person doing this? What is it about? What is the meaning? And then you have to make room for artistic intuition and inspiration. "Leave the glove on; don't ask me why I'm leaving it on . . . just leave it on!" The director is the ultimate clearing house for all this stuff!

Director Nicholas Meyer was interviewed in his office at ABC Circle Films, where he is busily at work on his next project. Whatever the nature of Mr. Meyer's projects, one thing is certain: they will always emerge as intriguing, artistic entities, due to the dedicated and energetic nature of the man. Nicholas Meyer's contributions to *Star Trek II* were many and diversified. His most significant contribution, however, was his presence, which transfused portions of his vital energy into the production staff of the film and into the movie itself.

Special Effects

Science fiction films can be described as historical travelogues to times that have not yet occurred and worlds that wait to be discovered. They are very different from other period films such as westerns and swashbucklers because the makers of those movies can always find locations and vehicles to use. Space operas, however, must manufacture their vehicles, their destinations and all points in between. This is where the wizards known as special photographic effects people enter the picture.

Preliminary Planning

Star Trek II was extremely lucky to have Robert Sallin as its producer. Because of his background in directing and producing hundreds of commercials, most on tight deadlines and budgets, many containing visual effects, he had a distinct advantage over most other producers. As Mr. Sallin points out, "Many of the people producing pictures like this don't know anything about special photographic effects. So they don't even know how to begin to attack the problems."

Sallin's expertise resulted in his being given the all-important responsibility of planning and coordinating the effects. He recalls:

The whole design, execution and placement of the special effects sequences in this picture . . . I did almost totally alone, largely because I know it, I understand it, I know how

113

Model maker Susan Pastor with the finished landscape of Gamma Regula

to deal with it, and because nobody else had time for it, anyway.

From the beginning, the element of time loomed over the heads of the *Star Trek II* production staff. Fortunately Sallin, who boarded the *Enterprise* in April, 1981, had help in the person of art director Michael Minor, who joined the staff two months after the producer.

Minor, who had done some freelance work for the *Star Trek* television series, designed all the storyboards for the film. Due to changes in the successive drafts of scripts written for the movie, Sallin had to tackle at least three completely different sets of effects boards, which Minor drew.

Finally, the go-ahead was given on a final approach to the script, and producer Sallin began the next stage of his work.

"When we got the go-ahead, I sat down and made a master chart that detailed every single special effects shot, and every single optical (effects) element that went into them."

The chart system designed by the producer was extremely elaborate. Nothing was being left to chance; now was the time to understand everything that had to be done so that costs could be held within the prescribed budget. At first the plan was to split up the effects responsibilities among several optical houses. Before this could be done, it had to be determined who could do each of the prescribed tasks for the least amount of money. To establish these decisions, Sallin brought his charting system into play and held bidding meetings. He elaborates:

> . . . We sat down with representatives from a number of special effects houses from all over the city and individually went through the storyboards frame by frame, element by element, second by second. It took upwards of three hours, each time, to do this. Then we received back from each company a detailed statement of what it would cost, how they would go about doing it and a schedule.

This ultra-detailed planning is not the norm in Hollywood, as indicated by the favorable reactions heaped upon the producer:

. . . A number of them told me that they had never, ever gotten this kind of detailed presentation and information to bid on . . . *ever*.

To assist him in evaluating the submitted bids, Mr. Sallin called in a consultant. He picked the multitalented effects expert, Jim Danforth, with whom he was familiar from the days when they had worked on commercials together. Sallin remembers:

I brought him in at the time when I was considering splitting up the work; I was considering Jim as a possible candidate for special effects supervisor, someone who would answer to me and keep it all coordinated and running.

Unfortunately, this collaboration never came about, but the producer was nevertheless able to consult Danforth, an artist for whom he has great respect:

Jim is an Academy Award–winning nominee, and a very knowledgeable guy. . . . As I was getting my bids in, I paid Jim and said, "You go off now and bid this show for me, and give me a schedule." And he did, without seeing my bids . . . so I had a basis of comparison.

The more definite the information that poured in, and the more that *Star Trek II*'s deadlines loomed closer, the clearer it became that effects responsibilities could not be spread thinly around the city to unconnected facilities. The producer recalls:

As our schedule kept being pushed back, in terms of beginning production, it became very apparent to me that I really couldn't do the special effects with a variety of houses. . . . The schedule began to get to me. It was then that I realized that I was going to have to put the job all under one roof if we had any chance at all of making the release date. So that suddenly limits you severely. I narrowed it down to a few major effects houses, and . . . then I met with the ILM people. . . .

Industrial Light and Magic

When Sallin joined the staff of the film, ILM had taken out an ad in one of the film industry's trade papers. The producer had pinned it up on his wall, impressed by the list of pictures credited to the effects house. At that time, he called the advertisement to the attention of executive producer Bennett, who had resisted the idea of using them because the firm was located many miles away from Los Angeles, in San Rafael. But after it was decided that a self-contained facility was needed, it was almost inevitable that the contract would be awarded to them. The company, after all, had been founded to meet the specialized needs of another famous motion picture project having much the same types of visual challenges: *Star Wars* (20th Century-Fox, 1977).

The saga of Industrial Light and Magic company began in June, 1975, when filmmakers George Lucas and Gary Kurtz were attempting to determine how they could translate the outer space action elements of their film *Star Wars* to the motion picture screen in a convincing manner, on time and on budget. The two contacted John Dykstra, an optical effects expert who had previously worked with fellow wizard Doug Trumbull. Dykstra concluded that *Star Wars* needed a self-contained visual effects facility that would handle all the operations necessary to accomplish the complicated spaceship dogfights.

ILM first came together in a warehouse in Van Nuys, California, in the San Fernando Valley. In eight months, the empty storage facility was converted into a visual magic shop in which the need for specialized equipment predetermined the individual departments that would be required.

The departments set up were capable, properly combined and coordinated, of doing everything needed in *Star Wars*. There were:

1) A Model Shop to design and construct the miniatures of spaceships, entire planets and their weird inhabitants

2) A Carpentry Shop which built and modified special camera, editing, animation and projection equipment

3) The Machine Shop, which constructed the specially required equipment

4) An Electronics Shop to devise the all-important "motion control" camera and control system

5) A Rotoscope Department to produce mattes and explosion-enhancement footage

6) The Optical Printing Department, which combined the needed multiple images onto single pieces of motion picture film, and

7) The Film Control Department, which filed and coordinated the special effects film elements.

Previous to *Star Wars*, only an experimental handful of shots in scattered science fiction and fantasy films had attempted to depict spaceships that moved fluidly among the stars. To fill his need, Dykstra supervised the design and construction of the complex machine named after him. The "Dykstraflex" featured a series of motors that controlled seven axes of movement. Combined, these patterns could make it appear that ships were darting toward each other in movements that could be duplicated as many times as needed to film a completed shot. Construction on this historic machine began in July, 1975.

During production of *Star Wars*, a maximum of 75 people were employed. Two full shifts of artists worked continuously during post-production to finish their monumental task of producing the 360 separate special visual effects shots seen in the film.

The miniatures produced for *Star Wars* ranged in size from 1-inch-high representations of the film's robots, C3PO and R2D2, to a detailed surface area of the "Death Star" that measured 1600 square feet. Some models also had to be mass-produced, and a variety of molding techniques was used to produce the total of 75 miniatures required for the film's production.

Almost two full years were needed to fully develop the ILM facilities and accomplish the *Star Wars* work. Key developments included novel contributions to accomplish "blue screen" photography more convincingly than it had ever been produced before.

The completed facility had been moved first to San Anselmo, California, and then to San Rafael, near San Francisco.

Planning

ILM was the answer to *Star Trek II*'s problems in the areas of visual effects and certain physical effects. Producer Sallin recalls the beginnings of the necessary conferences with ILM personnel:

> We awarded the job to ILM. Because of our schedule, we had actually started our pre-production meetings prior to our director being selected. Then Nick [Nicholas Meyer] came aboard, and he attended one meeting at ILM, and that was it; it was more of a review meeting than anything else.

The remainder of the time, Sallin himself shuttled between Industrial Light and Magic and Stages 5, 8, and 9 at Paramount Studios. At ILM, he discovered a highly skilled individual with whom he had something in common:

> I asked ILM to do a number of things that we used to do in the commercial world. Funnily enough, Rose Duignan came from commercials, too, although she had worked on *Star Wars*.

Sallin's requests involved methods that would provide continuous and complete accounts of the expenses and progress involved in *Trek II*'s effects:

> . . . I asked for weekly status reports from every department: animation, camera, model, mattes, opticals, number of shots to be done, number of shots attempted, number of shots completed . . . They were terrific, also in terms of money. They said we would have a dollar-by-dollar analysis at the end of each weekly report as to where we stood. If I dropped a shot, I wanted the credit to show. If I added one, I wanted its cost reflected in the report, so I would always know . . . no surprises.

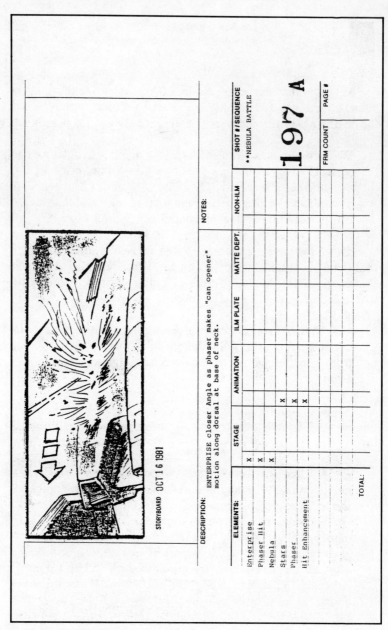

A storyboard for a battle scene special effect. The *Enterprise* is damaged by the *Reliant*'s phasers.

Oversize section of the *Enterprise* is burned frame by frame by animator Ken Ralston

An optical phaser effect completes the illusion of the *Enterprise* suffering heavy structural damage

The Miniatures

There *were* surprises, but they were all pleasant ones. The talented folks at ILM handled all spaceship shots that were not stock shots taken from the first *Star Trek* feature. These obligations included furnishing the backgrounds, such as planets and nebulas, and devising the means to show the destruction of portions of the *Enterprise* and the *Reliant* without actually damaging the valuable miniatures.

To accomplish these illusions of destruction, large sections of the *Enterprise* and *Reliant* were built. The *Enterprise* engineering section, with its attached pylon leading to the saucer section, was fabricated from various materials. Those portions scheduled for demolition were constructed of wax. The damages were inserted gradually by a special effects artist working with sculpting tools. Within the section, lighting equipment provided the beginnings of the phaser damage's explosive results. To complete the illusion, ILM opticals later inserted other explosion elements, as well as the phaser beam that caused all the damage.

The *Reliant* damage was inflicted in much the same manner. The ship's "roll bar" was constructed as a large-scale miniature. This breakaway model was filmed in front of a nebula background. As the phaser hits occurred, explosive charges were detonated and pre-packed pieces of plastic scrap were ejected. If the first take went wrong, the model would not have had to be constructed again from scratch; it was designed to be "destroyed" repeatedly, as many times as it would take to get the finished effect executed perfectly.

The *U.S.S. Enterprise* is the same one used during the production of *Star Trek: The Motion Picture*. Constructed by another company for the different demands of the first *Trek* feature film, the *Enterprise* is filled with complex circuitry. For shots in which the starship had to photograph smaller, ILM constructed other, smaller miniatures of the *Enterprise*, minus the complicated insides of the big one.

The *U.S.S. Reliant* is a starship of a slightly different variety, designed and constructed especially for *Star Trek II*. Input for the design of the ship was provided to *Star Trek II*'s production designer, Joseph R. Jennings, and art director, Michael Minor. The ship's designs were forwarded to ILM, where the model was built by Steve Gawley's model shop. Constructed from vacuformed plastic, the *Reliant* is much lighter than the *Enterprise*. Its interior wiring is also simpler than the *Enterprise*'s, since it contains only the workings to permit it to do exactly what was required of it in the *Star Trek II* script.

The *Reliant* interior contains a metal armature that permits it to be mounted in a variety of positions for filming. The ship, which contains most of the design features of the *Enterprise,* is a more consolidated version of her sister ship. The vessel is supposed to be a newer design, which is why her registration number is higher than that of the *Enterprise.* Undoubtedly she was assigned her number by a student of American history; her designation is "NCC-1864."

Space Lab Regula One, the site of the final research that led to the completion of Project Genesis, is another miniature left over from *Star Trek: The Motion Picture.* Producer Sallin suggested that ILM personnel invert the miniature, make some additions to it and film the revised edition for *Star Trek II.*

The planets seen in *Star Trek II* are also miniatures. The lifeless exterior of planet Gamma Regula, within which Khan maroons Captain Kirk, had two versions. For long shots a half-sphere was built, with an interior mounting bracket. Details of the landscape were painted on the outside of the semiglobe. For closeups, where texture was required, a 300-pound tabletop model was sculpted, then detailed.

The Mutara Nebula

The backgrounds of the film's space scenes were mostly created at ILM. The most significant of these were the scenes involving the Mutara Nebula. This purplish cloud of incandescent gas was added to the film for stylistic reasons, to provide a background more interesting than a multitude of stars and an occasional solar system.

Producer Robert Sallin elaborates on the evolution of the idea:

The problem I had to deal with, and Mike Minor helped solve it, was that I had this vision of these two ships battling in space. I kept saying to everybody that they are *not* highly manageable X-wing fighters, that it was going to be very boring seeing two lethargic galleons standing off and zapping each other at vast distances. I said we've got to put them in a strikingly different environment . . . something that hasn't been seen before. Well, Mike [Minor] had all these wonderful books, and he kept bringing them up to my office when we were working on the boards. And I remember looking at the cover of one of them and saying, "What's that?" And he said, "That's a nebula." I said, "A nebula, eh?" So the nebula emerged as the background, and I suggested to Harve that if we put the ships into the nebula, that would mean that the ships' viewscreens wouldn't work, and that their shields wouldn't work. That way they would both be even: Kirk's superior experience would then balance the superior fire power of the *Reliant*. And that's how the concept evolved.

The end result, as executed by the ILM artists, resembled a futuristic video-game background, always interesting, always fluid and iridescent.

The nebula effects were executed within a 4 foot by 8 foot aquarium, filled with a layer of fresh water beneath a layer of salt water. The two varieties of solutions create an "inversion layer" into which is pumped clouds of liquid latex. As the white latex floats free and creates abstract patterns within the tank, colored gels are used as lighting sources and the resulting shapes are photographed. The problem is that these shapes do not remain static, and there is no way to determine what sort of patterns will result at any given time. There is also no way to control them once they do form. All the patterns used, therefore, are produced by sheer chance. ILM personnel would watch for an especially interesting pattern to form, and then they would make it even more intriguing by shining moving lights on it and through it.

The technique of creating cloud effects within a tank was used most convincingly in *Close Encounters of the Third Kind*, and, in the opinion of ILM visual effects supervisor Ken Ralston, as far back as Paramount's 1956 film *The Ten Commandments*. To supplement this type of nebula effect, ILM artists also created paintings of the nebula interior. The painting variation of the effect was used during closeup photography of the explosive roll bar *Reliant* section.

Ceti Eels

Sitting on a table in producer Robert Sallin's living room, carefully imprisoned within a transparent plastic cage, is an extremely repugnant life form known as a Ceti Eel. The adult monster in the box is accompanied by two young offspring. In the film, it is the smaller (and slimier) varieties of monster that create two of the more horrifying moments ever to appear on screen: the entrance and exit of the little beasts into and out of Chekov's ear.

Earlier drafts of the *Star Trek II* script did not feature the Ceti Eels (the last surviving life form on planet Ceti Alpha V). Producer Bob Sallin recalls the evolution of the creatures:

> The earlier drafts of the script did not have the Ceti Eels in them. They had, instead, something that affixed itself to the back of the neck. And I kept saying to Harve [Bennett], "That's been done . . . it's boring." I said that what we needed was something that would get a really visceral reaction from the audience when it happened. I said we need something that's really slimy and just totally disgusting.

At this point, nature supplied the crucial assistance.

> The next day I happened to walk out my door, and what was walking across the walkway, but a slug. I looked at it, and I said, "That's *it!*" I went to Harve and said, "It's got to be like a slug," and he said, *"Terrific.* We'll call it a *Ceti Eel!"* I said, "That's not what it is," but he answered, "Well, call it that anyway." So it became the Ceti Eel.

With the visualization for the creatures arrived at, it remained for the imaginative folks at ILM to determine exactly what Ceti

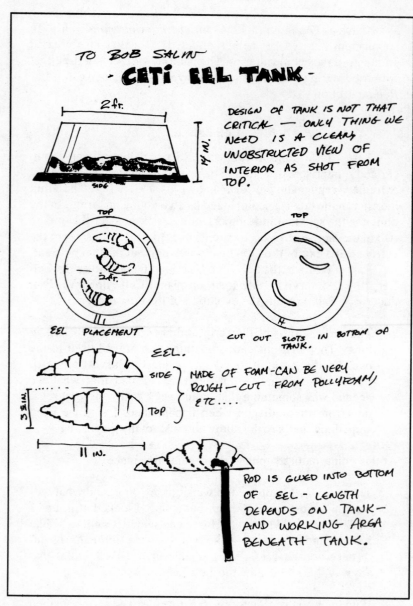

TO BOB SALIN

- CETI EEL TANK -

2 ft. · 14 IN.

SIDE

DESIGN OF TANK IS NOT THAT CRITICAL — ONLY THING WE NEED IS A CLEAN, UNOBSTRUCTED VIEW OF INTERIOR AS SHOT FROM TOP.

TOP

2 FT.

EEL PLACEMENT

TOP

CUT OUT SLOTS IN BOTTOM OF TANK.

EEL.

SIDE

TOP

MADE OF FOAM—CAN BE VERY ROUGH—CUT FROM POLLYFOAM, ETC....

3 3/4 IN.

11 IN.

ROD IS GLUED INTO BOTTOM OF EEL — LENGTH DEPENDS ON TANK — AND WORKING AREA BENEATH TANK.

Design sketches for the Ceti Eel and its tank

126

⌐CETI EEL TANK⌐

EELS ARE MOVED FROM UNDER SET—
AS THEY ARE DRAGGED BENEATH THE
PLASTIC— SAND ALSO MOVES, SWELLS, ETC.

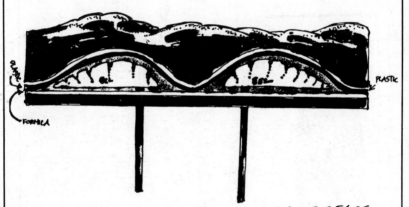

—WOOD BASE SHOULD HAVE FORMICA SURFACE—
ALSO WITH THE SLOTS CUT IN IT— EELS
ARE PLACED IN —RODS THRU SLOTS — A
TOUGH PLASTIC SHEET IS PLACED OVER
THEM [EDGES GLUED TO TANK BASE] AND
SAND LAYED OVER IT ALL * PLASTIC SHOULD
BE PAINTED TO MATCH SAND TO PREVENT
ANY OF IT SHOWING THRU SAND.

127

A sequence of storyboards showing the Ceti Eels and eel tank

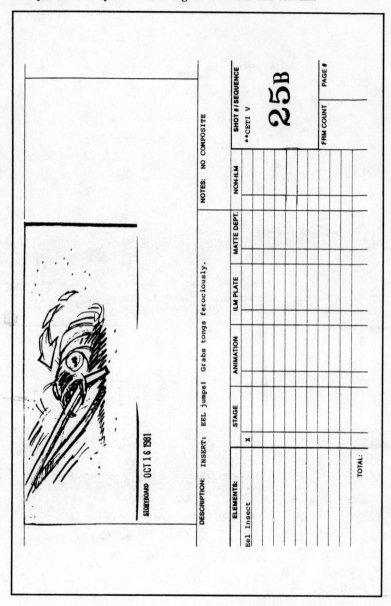

STORYBOARD OCT 16 1981

DESCRIPTION: INSERT: EEL jumps! Grabs tongs ferociously.

NOTES: NO COMPOSITE

SHOT #/SEQUENCE
**CETI V
25B

ELEMENTS:	STAGE	ANIMATION	ILM PLATE	MATTE DEPT.	NON-ILM	FRM COUNT	PAGE #
Eel Insect	x						
TOTAL:							

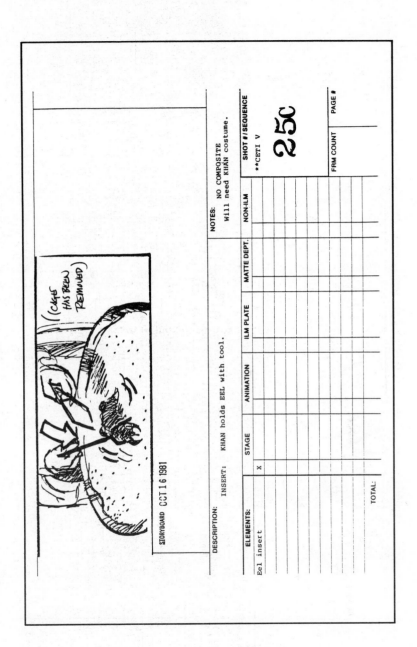

STORYBOARD OCT 1 6 1981

(CAPS HAS BEEN REMOVED)

NOTES: NO COMPOSITE
Will need KHAN costume.

DESCRIPTION: INSERT: KHAN holds EEL with tool.

ELEMENTS:	STAGE	ANIMATION	ILM PLATE	MATTE DEPT.	NON-ILM	SHOT #/SEQUENCE
Eel insert	X					**CETI V
						25c
TOTAL:						FRM COUNT PAGE #

129

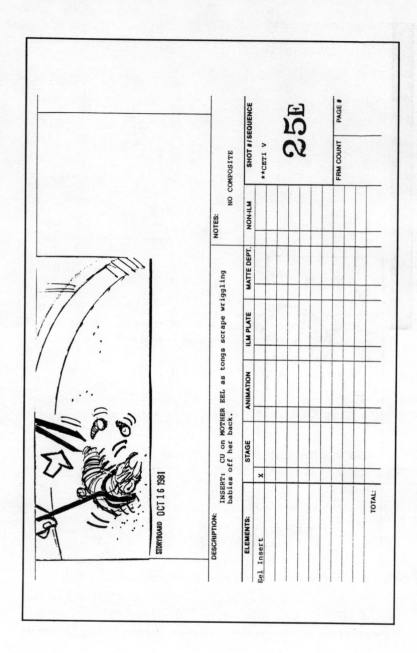

STORYBOARD OCT 16 1981

DESCRIPTION: INSERT: CU on MOTHER EEL as tongs scrape wriggling babies off her back.

NOTES: NO COMPOSITE

SHOT # / SEQUENCE
**CETI V
25E

ELEMENTS:	STAGE	ANIMATION	ILM PLATE	MATTE DEPT.	NON-ILM			
Eel Insert	X							
TOTAL:					FRM COUNT		PAGE #	

Ken Ralston manipulates the Ceti Eel in its cage

The adult Ceti Eel in its coat of artificial slime, held by a brave special effects staffer

131

Eels would look like and how they could be brought to life in their most nauseating form. Mr. Sallin recalls:

> I went to ILM and told them what I had in mind, the whole idea about it going in the ear, which they thought was great. Ken Ralston worked up lots of sketches, and we talked about what it did, how it grew—all that stuff. We finally came up with a design that we all liked, and they executed it wonderfully.

Popcorn vendors would probably disagree with Mr. Sallin's favorable opinion of the creatures; candy sales are bound to drop off whenever such repulsive creatures, so convincingly brought to life, influence audiences' appetites. The final version of the adult eels contain menacing yellow eyes, snapping pincer-type jaws, and body segments that appear to have been taken from a first cousin to *The Creature from the Black Lagoon*.

The Ceti Eels were actually puppets, operated from beneath with rods and other interior mechanisms. The tank was built with slots to permit this to be done. The baby eels were simpler affairs, cut almost in half, saturated with synthetic slime, and dragged slowly across the faces of actors Paul Winfield and Walter Koenig. The editing, sound effects and music aided the illusion.

In this sequence, Koenig got the full treatment of the little monster crawling into his ear and a much larger creature crawling out. To accomplish the chilling effect of the eel emerging, complete with added blood and screams, ILM constructed a large mockup of the actor's ear, complete with a section of jaw and sideburn. The section was constructed large enough so that the 14-inch model of the adult eel could be used in the scene. The super-large ear was sculpted from an actual casting of Koenig's own ear. This is probably the only time in the entire history of *Star Trek* that anyone's ear got more exposure than Leonard Nimoy's extended eartips.

Project Genesis

From the repulsive synthetic life form, the Ceti Eels, we journey to the Eden-like surroundings of the Genesis Cave beneath the "lifeless" planet Gamma Regula.

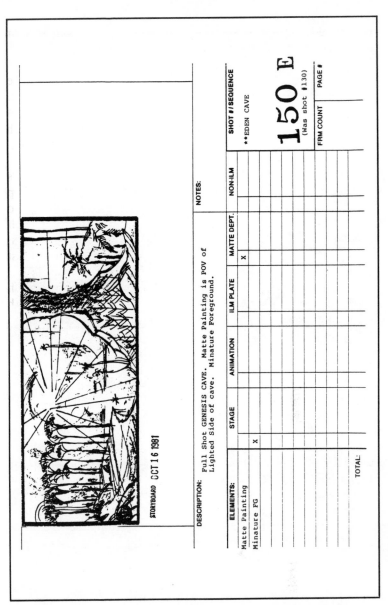

STORYBOARD OCT 1 6 1981

DESCRIPTION: Full Shot GENESIS CAVE. Matte Painting is POV of Lighted Side of cave. Minature Foreground.

NOTES:

SHOT #/SEQUENCE

150 E

**EDEN CAVE

(Was shot #130)

FRM COUNT   PAGE #

ELEMENTS:	STAGE	ANIMATION	ILM PLATE	MATTE DEPT.	NON-ILM
Matte Painting				X	
Minature FG	X				
TOTAL:					

Storyboards of the Genesis Cave in the heart of Gamma Regula

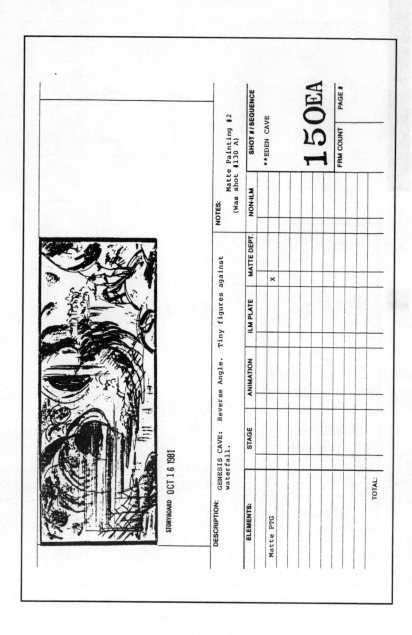

STORYBOARD OCT 1 6 1981

DESCRIPTION: GENESIS CAVE: Reverse Angle. Tiny figures against waterfall.

NOTES: Matte Painting #2
(Was shot #130 A)

SHOT #/SEQUENCE

**EDEN CAVE

150EA

ELEMENTS:	STAGE	ANIMATION	ILM PLATE	MATTE DEPT.	NON-ILM
Matte PTG				X	
TOTAL:					

FRM COUNT	PAGE #

134

The Eden Cave as painted by artist Frank Ordaz

Matte painter Chris Evans and the Eden Cave

Earlier drafts of the *Star Trek II* script featured "The Omega System," an incredibly powerful explosive with no constructive abilities whatsoever. It was mentioned, however, that the Omega explosive could completely destroy any planet. As the production evolved in complexity, the reasoning became that if Federation technology possessed the power to destroy worlds, perhaps it also possessed the ability to create them as well. Due to its ability to destroy existing life forms during the process of planet-wide renovation, the Genesis Torpedo is also a terrifying weapon. The final ending of the film, which implies that Mr. Spock may indeed someday return to life as a result of the life-giving forces of the Genesis Wave, would not have been possible without the complex idea of Project Genesis.

Project Genesis came about as the result of the film's art director, Michael Minor. Minor, a science fiction fan and a follower of the original *Star Trek* television series (and who also created the Melkot for "Spectre of the Gun" and some miscellaneous decorative artwork used during third-season episodes), recalled a word used in an episode of the series: "terraforming." Mentioning the concept to executive producer Harve Bennett, Minor found his idea instantly accepted.

Once Project Genesis became part of the script, it became necessary to bring it to life on motion picture film.

The set for the Genesis Cave entrance was designed to resemble a huge bubble, the idea of production designer Jennings and art director Mike Minor. Joseph Jennings reasoned that the energies released during the Genesis procedure would be capable of melting rock. The set, therefore, should look volcanic in nature. Minor remembered a 1953 science fiction film *Invaders from Mars,* in which production designer William Cameron Menzies had included caverns that were melted into the earth by Martian heat rays. The set featured hundreds of bubbles stuck into the walls and ceilings, to suggest that terrific heat had been present there. The original intention with the Genesis Cave was to have the matte paintings continue this style. The end result, however, featured only a few bubble shapes with a large surrounding area that suggests a Garden of Eden landscape more easily identifiable with the existence of life.

Only a comparatively small portion of the set was actually constructed: the entranceway, a few trees and a little surrounding ground. The remainder of the beautiful landscape is an optical painting. The moving waterfall was left partially blank in the painting, and behind the artwork a rotating cotton ball, properly lit and photographed, provided the illusion of flowing water. Chris Evans's main painting, photographed by Neil Krepela and Craig Barron, is a masterfully executed illusion. Two more paintings, a second by Evans and another by Frank Ordaz, complete the views of the Genesis interior.

We first see the potential of Project Genesis in the tape Kirk runs for Spock and McCoy. Earlier drafts of the script did not include this, but used a simpler type of demonstration of Genesis. Once again, creative collaboration and inspired effects personnel transformed a relatively pedestrian idea into an extremely dramatic moment in the film.

The Genesis Tape runs only slightly over one minute in length, but it nevertheless took a crew of ten artists almost six months to achieve. Alvy Ray Smith and Loren Carpenter headed the team that produced the tape, first conceived of by ILM visual effects supervisor Jim Veilleux. The final tape was produced as an animation drawn directly into a computer using a light-sensitive pen and a special screen. The final result is so fluid, and so vivid, that it almost appears as though it all happened out in space on location with a camera there to capture it on film. After seeing the footage, it's no wonder the United Federation of Planets decided to fund Dr. Carol Marcus's project.

Other Effects

In the interest of accuracy, it should be pointed out that ILM did not do *all* the optical effects seen in *Star Trek II: The Wrath of Khan*. Some effects were accomplished by effects artist Peter Kuran's company, Visual Concepts Engineering (VCE). Among these are the transporter effect and the glowing lights that signified Spock was being bombarded by lethal radiations during his death scene.

Cameraman Don Dow, head cameraman and supervisor Ken Ralston, and camera assistants Selwyn Eddy and Mike Owens in front of the closed tank in which the Mutara Nebula effects were generated

Model makers (left to right) Larry Tan, Bob Diepenbrock, Bill George, Jeff Mann, Martin Brenneis (electronics), Steve Sanders, Brian Chin, Mike Fulmer, Sean Casey, and Steve Gawley pose Western-style with the completed *Reliant* miniature

Head model maker Steve Gawley assembling the infrastructure of the
U.S.S. *Reliant* miniature

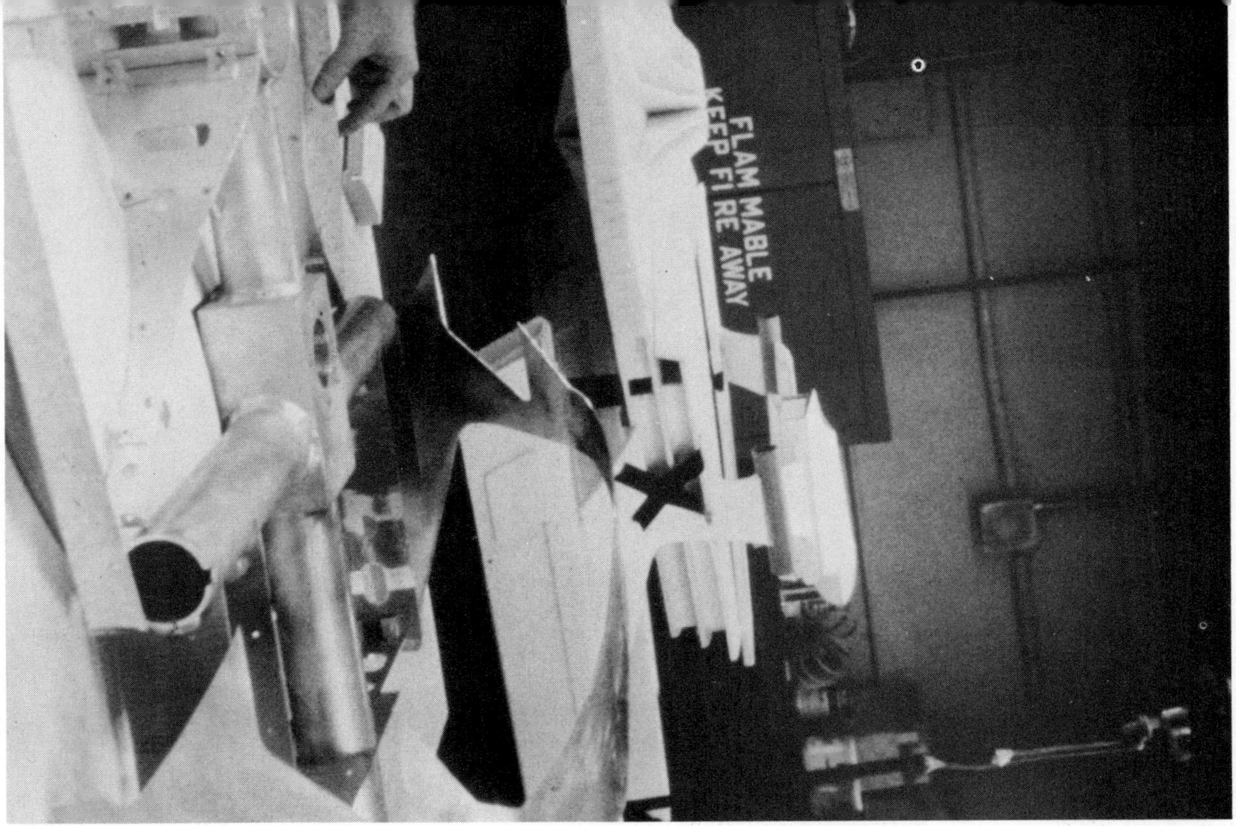

INDUSTRIAL LIGHT AND MAGIC

Camera Supervisor Jim Veilleux and the Gamma Regula space station miniature

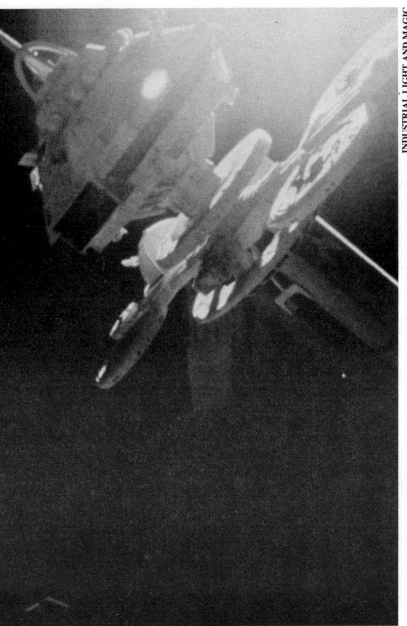

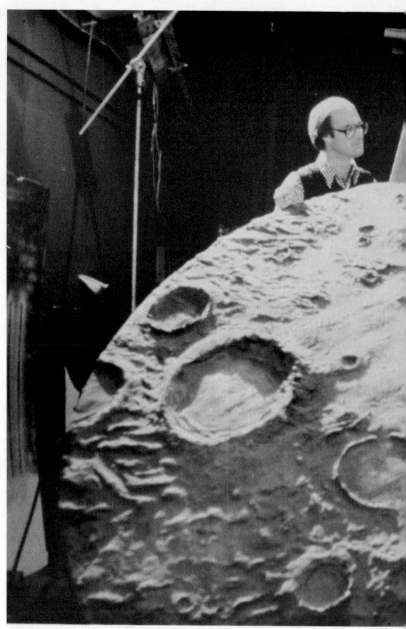

Close-up section of the planetoid Regula with ILM crew

Don Dow, Selwyn Eddy, and Ken Ralston set up the U.S.S. *Enterprise* model

INDUSTRIAL LIGHT AND MAGIC

Cameraman Scott Farrar lights up the U.S.S. *Enterprise* **model**

On location in Golden Gate Park, San Francisco, for the Genesis Planet sequence; the plant life was specially imported.

The new transporter effect is the most beautiful one ever presented. Combined with a "pillar of light" effect, not unlike that seen in *Forbidden Planet* (MGM, 1956), are twin bars of light, parallel to the ground, that gradually merge in the middle of the subject. For the first time, people are capable of moving while they're being transported. The company's original intent was to depict the transported individuals materializing gradually, beginning with skeleton, progressing to muscles, blood vessels and finally the skin and clothes. If done, it would have resembled effects seen in the motion picture *This Island Earth* (Universal, 1955), and in the *Outer Limits* television series episode, "The Special One." Producer Bob Sallin steered Peter Kuran away from this concept, and after much experimentation the final effect evolved.

The special effects in *Star Trek II* are beautiful and powerful, yet they fit in so smoothly with the live-action footage of the film that the audience need not think about them as special effects unless they wish to. They are not the core of the production; they enhance the live-action elements that are the film's central story. The ILM and non-ILM effects enable the audience to enjoy the visual wonders of space while traveling there with old friends.

Leonard Nimoy

Leonard Nimoy's office is a warm place, just as Nimoy himself is a warm individual. His office is filled with objects of art: photographs taken by Nimoy the photographer, posters advertising productions starring Nimoy the actor and testimonials to the skills of this multifaceted individual. Nimoy himself is filled with artistic knowledge and drives and a very potent sense of responsibility to honor the people and the skills that form the core of his life. He is an actor, a teacher, a husband and a father, and he manages to fill all these roles, as well as others, while occupying a place of honor in modern mythology as the man who brings Mr. Spock to life.

QUESTION—*When were you first approached to work in* Star Trek II?

LN — We started shooting in November . . . I think it must have been spring of last year . . . spring of '81.

Q — *What were your thoughts at the time?*

LN — My thoughts were the same as they've always been on *Star Trek* projects. I want to know what's the story, what is the script all about, who's writing it, who's directing it. I've always tried to be selective, not just about *Star Trek* but about anything I do. I've passed the point where I need the work, fortunately. If I have the opportunity to be more selective, that means I also have the responsibility to be

Leonard Nimoy in some Earth-style meditation between takes

more selective. And by that I mean if I'm out on a job and I don't like the script, or there's something else about the project that I don't like, and I'm on the job and I'm unhappy with the job, I have nobody to blame but myself, because I didn't have to take the work. So those are my thoughts—what it's all about, what we are doing.

Q — *What was your working relationship with Nicholas Meyer?*

LN — He's a terrific guy. Tremendous energy and very, very bright. I would say probably there are two sides to the coin when you're working with Nick in that he has a wonderful, childlike energy and excitement about what he does, and it's very infectious. At the same time, that same childlike quality can sometimes be exasperating, but I got along with him wonderfully. I found him sometimes very obstinate when he believed that he was right about a point, and often he was. But at the same time he was really willing to listen to your point of view, and in a number of cases would say, "Let me think about that." And a couple of days later he would come back and say, "I think you're right, let's do it that way," about something that had to be done a week hence. I have no negative feelings about Nick at all . . . I really enjoyed working with him.

Q — *Did you have much creative input yourself, as an actor and director?*

LN — I try to let the director shoot his own picture. If I think there's a moment that he perhaps isn't seeing, that he may be missing, I might point that out to him. And if I can be helpful in that sense, I might make a suggestion here and there. I might say, "Gee, there's a thing happening over here that you might want to get a little closer on or something. Maybe if you move the camera around you'll see it a little bit better." But when you walk in to stage a scene, there are a number of elements that have to come together, including attitude and performance, positioning of the actors and positioning of the camera. And to a certain extent the actor will adapt what he's doing based on where the camera is. In some cases, if adapting to where the camera is creates a problem within the staging of the scene, then one might say, "This is really the way I should do this, physically, but you won't see it if the camera's there. Is it possible to move the camera?" So there's always that kind of give and take with any director.

Q — *What was Mr. Meyer's reaction to your straightening of the jacket during Spock's death scene?*

LN — I don't remember that he commented on it. There was some concern, I understand, when it was first previewed—I wasn't there—because there was a little bit of a laugh at that moment.

Leonard Nimoy is most un-Spockian during a rehearsal break

Q — *I think it's a very nervous laugh. Are people worried about Spock?*

LN — Yes, you're right. And the nervousness leads to two different possible interpretations of what that laughter is about. . . . There are two kinds of reactions. . . . Those who believe that the worst is already over and that he's okay, that it is a mistake or whatever, I think they have a little release laughter when they see Spock get himself together. On the other hand, I think a lot of people were very moved by Spock straightening his jacket, because it's the other. He's on his way to die and wants to be in proper shape for it, wants to be orderly about it.

Q — *There was a* Mission: Impossible *episode, "The Choice," in which you were a Rasputin-type character named Votrane. You graveled your voice, and it was very similar to the voice you used speaking to Kirk through the wall in the reactor room.*

LN — That's interesting; I hadn't made that connection. In this particular case it came out of my thinking that probably one of the things that would be happening to Spock in that radiation chamber would be that he was quickly dehydrating, and when that happens to you the vocal cords tend to get very dry and raspy. I've had it happen to me personally where you get very dry, so that's how I arrived at that. I just suggested by the sound that there was something wrong here; I didn't want him sounding healthy at that point.

Q — *Weren't you also doing subtle breathing things during that scene, too, to denote that Spock was in great pain?*

LN — I was trying to; I hope it communicates. You know, some of these things do and some of them don't, but some are useful to the actor and therefore serve the scene, and some are not only used for the actor, but communicated well. I was really trying to come to grips with internal damage and internal pain, beyond what we could see, and as a result the speech pattern became the kind of thing you do when you're

In another angle of a portrait-take, Leonard Nimoy breaks into spontaneous laughter; the unreleased version.

preoccupied with controlling some aspect of the body and trying to speak at the same time. That's what that was all about.

Q — *How do you think they'll handle the next picture, regarding Mr. Spock?*

LN — There are various ways to approach it. You could deal with a reincarnation or resurrection very quickly, and a temporarily aberrated form of some kind that has to be transmuted back to what we recognize as Spock. You could do a picture on the other side. You could do a story where you take the audience into that existence where Spock is now. You have the regenerating effect of the Genesis Planet functioning on that body, and suppose that body is regenerating, and suppose that during that regenerative pro-

159

cess we find a way to the other side, experience what Spock is going through during that process and where he is, who he's seeing, who he's talking to, what he is experiencing. What is he thinking? Does he *want* to go back? You have a lot of distinct possibilities, so you play the other side of the existence before you bring him back, assuming you're going to. You could also do a picture about Spock in which he hardly appears. You could have this wonderful adventure dealing with the question of what the planet's effect is on Spock's body, with everybody realizing there's a potential resurrection here at the very end of the film. So you could do any one of three approaches, or even more; there are a lot more. It's a question of execution. In this particular project, in the next one, my feeling is that there are a lot of wonderful tracks laid down, and it's a question of choosing one and executing it very, very well. I don't have any doubt that a wonderful story could be written, that there are wonderful stories available to be written. It's just a matter of execution.

Q — *Have you ever given any thought to submitting a storyline?*

LN — I have given it some thought, and when the right time comes, if I'm given the opportunity, I would enjoy sitting down and discussing it, just as you and I are discussing right now the various possibilities that I perceive. It would be very wonderful if I could be involved at that level.

Q — *How do you feel about people tending to confuse you and Spock as the same entity?*

LN — I really don't think it's true anymore. I find, time and time again, on the street, in elevators, in restaurants, airplanes, public situations, people call me by name. I just don't think it's true anymore. And maybe that's why I've reached the point in my life where Spock and *Star Trek* have taken their proper place in my career, you see. Once in a while I'll still get somebody yelling "Spock" down the street with a wild

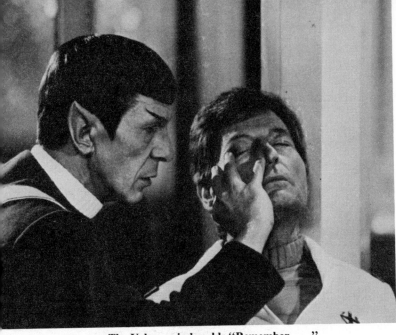

The Vulcan mind-meld: "Remember . . ."

laugh and a wave, but it doesn't bother me. I do find that I have established my own identity strongly enough that I don't have to be concerned about it.

Q — *Have you been having any repeated reactions by the fans when you've been on publicity tours for this movie? Do people ever approach you and say one thing over and over?*

LN — About this particular film? Sure. They all want to know what's going to happen next to Spock. Sure. And I think the best one of all is that three weeks ago I was in New York, and coming back here I went to the airport counter to check in, and the lady behind the counter said, "Mr. Nimoy, do you die in the *Star Trek* movie?" And I said, "Well, I think you're going to have to see the picture," and she said, "I did."

Q — *What was the purpose of your saying "Remember?" after giving Dr. McCoy the Vulcan neck-pinch?*

LN — I'm intrigued with the magic games you can play with the Vulcan character. I always have been. One of the earliest, most effective acting lessons that I received from Jeff Corey and from reading Stanislavsky and from all the people whom I admired and who helped me learn to be an actor was that you learn the differences between your character and everybody else's. Study those differences and use them. The differences are what make us individuals. Well, with a Vulcan there are all kinds of differences to play, and all kinds of differences to be discovered, if you keep an open mind. And that's the magic of the Spock character. . . . The point of doing it is its very ambiguity. It is not literal and does not call for literal explanation. I thought that in doing it, I could simply be saying to him, "Remember me," but if I leave the "me" off, it makes it magical. This also plants . . . the seeds for future possibilities if we were to use it . . ."

Q — *What do you think they may do with it in the next script?*

LN — There are a number of possibilities as well. For example, one that occurs to me—I hate to be giving all my storylines away—has to do with certain scientific information that Spock may be anticipating McCoy will need. Not only about Genesis, but—you know, there's a lot of room for exploration here. You have, again working on the differences of the character, a half-human, half-Vulcan anatomy here, and this is probably the doctor who will be on the case, if there is a case. And in that moment—"Remember. . . "—he may be computerlike, pouring into McCoy's brain certain knowledge of his own anatomy and chemistry that may be vital later . . . properly tickled in some wonderful, dramatic way McCoy will remember. But there's all kinds of great stuff to play. That's what's fun about the exploration, and that's what leads me to a very important point. We have discovered that by taking a chance and going over the edge or seeming to jump off a cliff, we have jumped into tremendously fertile territory. But I'm not playing it safe, really. I've taken the chance. I've said this is it, we're really doing it, folks, this is no joke, you are not being toyed with. If you feel deeply about it, let the tears flow, get it out. This is a catharsis, get it out. And, in a sense, enjoy it. Ride with it, go with us, let's see what happens, what we can discover here. If we can move you, terrific. The main concern was that we make them believe it, really believe it, and not try and cheat them of that experience. What happens afterwards is something else again. But during the playing of that material, there was never any sense of any game going on here. We're really doing this. Let's get in and explore what happens when we really do it.

Q — *And there never was any alternate ending?*

LN — Not that I know of. I certainly wasn't involved in an alternate ending. But you see, before the film opened, and before I had seen it, I really didn't know what it played like. I knew that we had filmed a death scene. I was not in the funeral scene, obviously. I was not in the scene that Bill played with his son. I was not in the bridge scene when they're all gathering together to talk about how they feel about what has just happened. So until I saw it, with an audience, there was no way of knowing what the emotional curve of that ending was going to be. Whether you end on a high note, a depressed note, whatever. So when I was asked to talk about it, I really couldn't be specific. I said, I haven't seen the picture, I don't know what you come away with yet. I'd get it from Harve on the phone. He'd say oh, we have this, and we have that and boy, they cry at this and you have a little release here, you know. Still, if you don't experience it first hand, it's hard to tell. And when I saw it with an audience, I loved it. I loved it. I thought, they're buying it, and it works, and it's good stuff.

Q — *Do you recall any specific incidents that took place during production?*

LN — The one startling thing that happened the day that we were shooting that radiation scene . . . I can't believe the shock

Leonard Nimoy with his best elfish grin

waves that went through me. I didn't want to shoot that scene. I mean, I was getting so tense and so emotional about that scene, I was looking for an excuse not to shoot it. And the tension and the concern was spreading, I could feel it. Everybody was affected by it; my God, we're going to shoot the scene where Spock dies. It's really pretty heavy stuff, you know. If you let yourself be in the least bit sentimental about the character and everything else, you think this could be the end. Nick and I had agreed about the cracked skin, and so forth, and that there might be some evidence of blood and that it would be green, Spock's blood being green, and since I had planned to put my hand on the glass to Bill, it seemed appropriate that there be a crack in the palm and there would be a trickle of green blood that would get on the glass. A dangerously melodramatic thing to do, but it might work. And that was transmitted to the makeup man, who was standing by, ready to put the glove on top of it, and take the glove off in the scene, revealing the bleeding hand. And here we are in this very tense situation, about to shoot the scene, and I looked around, and there's Werner Keppler; brilliant, brilliant craftsman. "Werner, you got the green, the blood?" "Yeah." And I'm looking off, talking to somebody, last-minute discussion with Bill, and I take a look . . . and my hand is now completely covered with green pancake. Completely covered. He had taken a sponge and gone to the pancake, wet it and got the stuff on a sponge. . . . He had missed the point, didn't understand what we were trying to do. Now, what's really funny about that is that Werner Keppler did the makeup on *The Incredible Hulk*. . . . Looking back, it's hilarious, but it's a very tense thing that happened. . . ."

Q — *Are you still teaching acting?*

LN — No. I still have all my teaching files. I refuse to dump them because I still think that someday I'll get back to it, but I just haven't had the time.

Q — *Does Mr. Spock have a tremendous international follow-ing?*

LN — Yeah, it's nice. I tell you, there's nothing quite like pene-trating the audience's imagination and being acceptable to such a wide range of people . . . different cultures, different styles, different attitudes.

Q — *What does your family think about the fame enjoyed by your character, Mr. Spock?*

LN — Well, I think we're all very proud of it. We see it as a success. I've had my share of artistic failures, where you do what you feel is very important and nobody cares. Everybody has, in our business. But [on *Star Trek*] I have always felt that we have been doing work in an entertain-ment form which has some substance and some food for thought. That's accomplishing a lot. Most of the things that I see done, certainly on television, I say to myself I wouldn't want to be in that; I wouldn't want to. And I'm certainly feeling for the actors who have to. You have to work, you know. But I wouldn't want to be in most of it. . . . I feel I'm blessed; and we all do. We have a terrific life. We have our personal, day-to-day problems just like any other family does, but boy, it's sure nice to know that we have public recognition and financial security for the rest of our lives. And we're very grateful for that. I consider myself a very lucky actor. And I know my family would say, "No, you're a very talented actor." They're very supportive. And I say, "Well, okay, but there're a lot of other talented people around, too, who don't have this kind of recognition and financial security, and they have to struggle all their lives, wondering when will I work again? I didn't enjoy it when I was in that condition twenty years ago.

Ricardo Montalban

Ricardo Montalban was born in Mexico City, Mexico, on November 25. Shortly after his birth, his family moved to Torreon, a city in Northern Mexico (north of Durango and south of Chihuahua). Montalban's early education was acquired in a Torreon parochial school. During this phase of his life, he was interested in becoming an engineer.

Ricardo's older brother, Carlos, had already emigrated to the United States when, at his family's urging, Ricardo came to this country and took up residence in Los Angeles, California. He enrolled in Hollywood's Fairfax High School; he was the oldest pupil there.

The five-feet eleven-inch Montalban appeared in many Fairfax High School plays, and while he was acting in one of these an MGM talent scout spotted him and suggested he take a screen test after his graduation. In the future, Ricardo would appear in many films produced at that studio, but his screen test would be delayed a few years at the urging of his brother.

Carlos had in the meantime moved to New York City; he felt that if his brother wished to begin a serious acting career, Manhattan was the place for him. Due to Carlos's glowing reports of the heart of the theater, Ricardo moved east. That was when he saw Broadway for the first time, and the glitter of the Great White Way obliterated all thoughts of attending college.

Responding to the attraction of the stage, Ricardo first obtained small stage roles. His own magnetic stage presence, how-

167

ever, soon elevated him above most of the other young Broadway hopefuls. In 1939 he landed his first important stage role, with actress Tallulah Bankhead in a summerstock production of *Her Cardboard Lover.*

Montalban's other New York roles put him opposite other stage celebrities: Elsa Maxwell in *Our Betters* and Ann Sten in *Nancy's Private Affair.*

While in New York, Ricardo also appeared in his first film, a Soundies short entitled *He's a Latin from Staten Island,* in which he played a guitar and performed a rendition of "A Latin from Manhattan" (a song made famous by Al Jolson).

Ricardo returned to Mexico after his mother died. There, he continued his acting career, performing in a total of thirteen motion pictures. Two of these features are *Santa* and *La Fuga.* Both were produced in 1943 and directed by Norman Foster. Foster was then married to Sally Blaine, Loretta Young's sister.

During his career in his native land, he won the Mexican equivalent of the Academy Award. Recognized as a fine artist in his native land, he decided to return to the United States and attempt to break into the Hollywood film scene. In 1945 Ricardo relocated to Los Angeles and signed a contract with Metro-Goldwyn-Mayer.

Montalban's first feature for MGM was *Fiesta.* Released in July, 1947, it was directed by Hollywood veteran Richard Thorpe (who had previously directed entries in the studio's *Tarzan* and *Thin Man* series). The movie co-starred Montalban with Esther Williams, Cyd Charisse, Mary Astor and Akim Tamiroff.

In 1953, Ricardo's MGM contract ran out, and the studio did not renew it. The actor once recalled, "That studio spoiled me for eight years. They didn't renew my contract and I felt completely alone and afraid."

This was a trying time for the performer, who found it difficult at first to find work outside of the super-studio's sheltering environment. It was during this time that the actor's religious faith helped to sustain him through his frustrations. Refusing to give up, Ricardo began to find parts that showcased his unique, wide range. His wonderful ability to be believable as an Oriental, an Indian, a Native American and other exotic types was one

Portrait of the archenemy: Ricardo Montalban as Khan

A light moment on the set for *Star Trek II*

factor that led him to be cast for the role of Khan Noonian Singh in one of *Star Trek*'s 1967 episodes, "Space Seed."

One of Montalban's first starring television roles was in a 1952 segment of the dramatic anthology series, *Chevron Theatre*. The episode was called "The Secret Defense of 117" and was the first science fiction television script written by Gene Roddenberry, who would create *Star Trek* a dozen years later.

The actor's intense portrayal of Khan in "Space Seed" brought the twentieth-century Sikh warrior-prince vividly to life in the era of the starship *Enterprise* and paved the way for his starring role in *Star Trek II: The Wrath of Khan*. It was but one of the actor's outstanding, magnetic performances.

In 1978, Ricardo won an Emmy Award for his appearance as an aging Native American in the miniseries, *How the West Was Won*. The actor, currently popular with television audiences as Mr. Roarke, the mysterious host to guests on *Fantasy Island,* has some very definite thoughts about the medium of television.

Television destroyed a way of life in Hollywood, and at first I resented it. For old-line movie people, television killed the red carpet. And yet it's to television that I owe my freedom from the bondage of the Latin Lover roles. Television came along and gave me parts to chew on. It gave me wings as an actor.

During his busy career, Montalban also co-starred on Broadway with Lena Horne in *Jamaica*. A musical comedy with music by Harold Arlen and lyrics by E.Y. Harburg, it boasted a record $1,500,000 in advance sales. When the play opened on October 13, 1957, the actor received good reviews despite the fact that the fantastic Ms. Horne usually overshadows her co-stars on stage.

Montalban has appeared in more than fifty motion pictures and in more than 100 roles in television productions (not counting his *Fantasy Island* episodes).

Fantasy Island has never been quite explicit in conveying the truth about the enigmatic and fun-loving Mr. Roarke. At first it appeared that he used various techniques of trickery, hypnotism and theatricalities to produce his illusions. Then, after Roarke's wife (now departed) and daughter were introduced into the series format, it began to appear that he was something considerably more than human. Possibly thousands of years old, with literally magical powers, Roarke even fought the devil on his series, and won.

In real life, Montalban states that he has no fantasies because the realities of his life have given him all the happiness that any man needs.

Ricardo Montalban's Credits

STAGE

Accent on Youth (1975)
Don Juan in Hell (Tour, 1972-73)
Her Cardboard Lover
Jamaica (Broadway, 1957)
King and I, The
Our Betters
Private Affair
Seventh Heaven (Broadway, 1955)

MOTION PICTURES

Across the Wide Missouri (Metro-Goldwyn-Mayer, 1951)
Battleground (Metro-Goldwyn-Mayer, 1950)

Khan in desert gear

Blue (Paramount, 1968)
Black Pirate, The (Italian, *Gordon il Pirata Nero,* 1961)
Border Incident (Metro-Goldwyn-Mayer, 1949)
Cadetes de la Naval (Mexican, 1944)
Casa de la Zorra, La (Mexican, 1943)
Cheyenne Autumn (Warner Brothers, 1964)
Cinco Fueron Escogidos (Mexican, 1942)
Conquest of the Planet of the Apes (20th Century-Fox, 1972)
Deserter, The (Paramount, 1971)
Desert Warrior (1961)
Escape from the Planet of the Apes (20th Century-Fox, 1970)
Fantasia Ranchera (Mexican, 1943)
Fiesta (Metro-Goldwyn-Mayer, 1947)
Fuga, La (Mexican, 1943)
Hemingway's Adventures of a Young Man (20th Century-Fox, 1962)
He's a Latin from Staten Island (Soundies short subject, 1941)
His Only Song (1948)
Hora de la Verdad, La (Mexican, 1944)
Joe Panther (Cougar, 1978)
Kissing Bandit, The (Metro-Goldwyn-Mayer, 1949)
Last Three Days of Pancho Villa, The (1973)
Latin Lovers (Metro-Goldwyn-Mayer, 1954)
Let No Man Write My Epitaph (Columbia, 1960)
Life in the Balance, A (20th Century-Fox, 1955)
Long Flight, The (1963)
Love is a Ball (United Artists, 1963)
Madame X (Universal, 1966)
Mark of the Renegade (Universal, 1951)
Money Trap, The (Metro-Goldwyn-Mayer, 1965)
My Man and I (Metro-Goldwyn-Mayer, 1952)
Mystery Street (Metro-Goldwyn-Mayer, 1950)
Neptune's Daughter (Metro-Goldwyn-Mayer, 1949)
Nosotros (Mexican, 1944)
On an Island with You (Metro-Goldwyn-Mayer, 1948)
Pepita Jimenez (Mexican, 1945)
Queen of Babylon (20th Century-Fox, 1956)
Rage of the Buccaneers (1962)

Razon de la Culpa, La (Mexican, 1942)
Reluctant Saint, The (Columbia/Royal Films Int'l., 1962)
Right Cross (Metro-Goldwyn-Mayer, 1950)
Santa (Mexican, 1943)
Saracen Blade, The (Columbia, 1954)
Sayonara (Warner Brothers, 1957)
Semiramis (Italian, 1955)
Singing Nun, The (Metro-Goldwyn-Mayer, 1965)
Sol Madrid (Metro-Goldwyn-Mayer, 1968)
Sombra (Metro-Goldwyn-Mayer, 1953)
Sombre Verde (1954)
Son of the Sheik (Italian/Spanish, 1957)
Spina Dorsale del Diavolo, La (1971)
Sweet Charity (Universal, 1968)
Three for Jamie Dawn (Allied Artists, 1956)
Three Musketeers, The (Mexican, 1941)
Train Robbers, The (Warner Brothers, 1972)
Two Weeks with Love (Metro-Goldwyn-Mayer, 1950)
Untouched (Excelsior, 1956)
Verdugo de Sevilla, El (Mexican, 1942)
Won Ton Ton, The Dog Who Saved Hollywood (Paramount, 1976)

TELEVISION

ABC Sunday Night Movie, The ("Fireball Foreward," 1972)
Adventures in Paradise ("The Derelict," 1959)
Alcoa Premiere ("The Glass Palace," 1963)
Alfred Hitchcock Theatre ("Outlaw In Town," 1960)
Alice Through the Looking Glass (NBC Special, 1966)
Aquarians, The (NBC, 1970)
Bell System Presents, The ("Captains Courageous," 1977)
Ben Casey ("Six Impossible Things Before Breakfast," 1963)
Black Water Gold (ABC Television Movie, 1970)
Bob Hope Chrysler Theatre ("Code Name Heraclitus," 1967)
     ("In Any Language," 1965)
     ("To Sleep, Perchance To Scream," 1967)
Bonanza ("Day of Reckoning," 1960)
Bracken's World ("Hey Gringo, Hey Chol," 1970)
(title unknown, 1969)

Burke's Law (title unknown, 1964)

(title unknown, 1965)

Chevron Theatre ("The Secret Defense of 117," 1952, by Gene Roddenberry)

Climax ("Island In the City," 1956)

("The Mojave Kid," 1955)

Columbo (title unknown, 1976)

Danny Thomas Show, The ("One For My Baby," 1968)

Defenders, The ("Whitewash," 1974)

Dick Powell Theatre ("Epilogue," 1963)

Dr. Kildare ("A Few Hearts, A Few Flowers," 1966)

("I Can Hear the Ice Melting," 1966)

Doris Day Show, The (title unknown, 1971)

Executive Suite (TV series regular playing David Valerio, CBS 1976-77)

Fantasy Island (ABC Television Movie, 1977)

Fantasy Island (TV series starring role as Mr. Roarke, ABC, beginning in 1978)

Felony Squad ("Blueprint For Dying," 1967)

(title unknown, 1968)

Ford Star Time ("Jeff McLeod, The Last Reb," 1960)

Ford Theatre (Cardboard Casanova," 1955)

("The Lady In His Life," 1956)

General Electric Theatre ("Estaban's Legacy," 1956)

Great Adventures ("Death of Sitting Bull," 1963)

("Pirate and Patriot," 1964)

Greatest Show on Earth, The ("Hanging Man," 1963)

Griff ("Countdown To Terror," 1973)

Gunsmoke ("Chato," 1970)

Hallmark Hall of Fame, The ("The Fantasticks," 1964)

Hawaii Five-O ("Death Wish On Tantalus Mountain," 1972)

("Samurai," 1968)

Here's Lucy (title unknown, 1972)

High Chapparral, The ("Our Lady of Guadalupe," 1968)

("Tiger By the Tail," 1968)

How The West Was Won (TV miniseries, 1978, Emmy Award)

Ironside ("The Sacrifice," 1968)

I Spy ("Magic Mirror," 1976)

It Takes a Thief ("Galloping Skin Game," 1968)
    ("Thingamabob Heist," 1968)
Lieutenant, The ("Tour of Duty," 1964, produced by Gene Roddenberry)
Lloyd Bridges Theatre ("War Song," 1962)
Longest Hundred Miles, The (1967)
Long, Hot Summer, The ("The Man With Two Faces," 1966)
Loretta Young Show, The ("At the Edge of the Desert," 1960)
    ("The Cardinal's Secret," 1956)
    ("Each Man's Island," 1959)
    ("Gina," 1955)
    ("The Hired Hand," 1960)
    ("The Man Who Couldn't Smile," 1961)
    ("The Man On Top," 1957)
    ("No Margin For Error," 1960)
    ("Rhubarb In Apartment 7-B," 1956)
Man From U.N.C.L.E., The ("The Dove Affair," 1964)
    ("The King of Diamonds Affair," 1966)
Marcus Welby, M.D. ("The Labyrinth," 1970)
Mark of Zorro, The (ABC Television Movie, 1974)
McCloud ("The Concrete Corral," 1970)
McNaughton's Daughter (TV series, 1976, recurring role as D.A. Charles Quintero)
Men From Shiloh, The ("Last of the Commancheros," 1970)
Mission: Impossible ("Snowball In Hell," 1967)
Name of the Game, The ("Echo of A Nightmare," 1970)
    ("Wrath of Angels," 1969)
NBC World Premiere Movie ("Desperate Mission," 1971—also called "Juan Murietta")
    ("Sarge: Badge Or Cross," 1971—pilot film)
NBC Friday Night Movies, The ("The Face of Fear," 1971)
New, Original Wonder Woman, The (ABC television movie, 1974)
Nichols ("The Seige," 1971)
O'Hara: U.S. Treasury ("Operation Lady Luck," 1972)
Pigeon, The (1969)
Playhouse Ninety ("Child of Trouble," 1957)
    ("Target For Three," 1959)
Play of the Week, The ("Rashomon," 1960)

Police Story ("Hard Rock Brown," 1977)
Return to Fantasy Island (ABC Television Movie, 1977)
Riverboat ("A Night At Trapper's Landing," 1959)
Rogues, The ("Mugger, Mugger By the Sea," 1964)
Slattery's People ("What Became of the White Tortilla?", 1964)
Star Trek ("Space Seed," 1967, Khan Noonian Singh)
Switch (title unknown, 1975)
Try to Catch a Saint (Universal Television Movie, date unknown)
20th Century-Fox Hour, The ("Broken Arrow," 1956)
     ("Operation Cicero," 1956)
Untouchables, The ("Strangle Hold," 1961)
Virginian, The ("The Big Deal," 1962)
     ("Wind of Outrage," 1962)
Wagon Train ("The Jean LeBec Story," 1957)
Wild Wild West, The ("The Night of the Lord of Limbo," 1966)
World of Disney ("Mustang," 1973, narrator)
     ("Zorro Auld Acquaintance," 1961)

William Shatner

William Shatner (Admiral James T. Kirk) has been within the last few years on stage in Los Angeles in *Cat on a Hot Tin Roof* and on the motion picture screen in the films *The Kidnapping of the President* and *Visiting Hours*. He also narrated the Oscar-winning documentary *Universe*.

On television, Shatner has added to his impressive list of credits by appearing in the 1977 syndicated miniseries *Testimony of Two Men* (as Adrian Ferrier), and the 1979 NBC miniseries *Little Women* (as Professor Friedrich Bhaer). In a funny, nostalgic moment, the actor also appeared as guest-star Captain Kirk on an episode of *Mork and Mindy*.

Shortly after Shatner appeared before the *Star Trek II* cameras, he began production of his new television series, *T. J. Hooker*. In the ABC show from Spelling-Goldberg Productions, he stars in the title role of a highly effective police officer. The series began running in January, 1982.

William Shatner has repeatedly demonstrated his versatility as an actor on stage, screen and television, portraying a wide variety of individual characters in everything from Shakespeare to westerns. His distinctive voice has been heard narrating films and giving dramatic readings on records. On television quiz shows, he's a welcome guest who is liable to produce extremely funny puns at any moment. Taking into account his long list of entertainment credits, Mr. Shatner is certainly one of the most remarkable performers of this century.

William Shatner: Admiral James T. Kirk

George Takei and William Shatner react to an unseen peril between takes

Dr. McCoy, Admiral Kirk, and Mr. Spock in a between-scenes portrait

"Let me show you something that will make you feel young . . . young as when the world was new . . .": William Shatner and Bibi Besch

Sulu, Kirk, Uhura, and McCoy on their way to the *Enterprise*

Shatner's most impressive artistic creation, though, is James T. Kirk. His many performances as this character supply the series' fans with their central point of human reference on the *Enterprise*.

Star Trek II presented a series of challenges for William Shatner. Kirk, now an Admiral, was coming to terms with his approaching middle age. Actor Shatner could easily have wanted nothing to do with such a scenario, but what happened was that he turned the film into a tour-de-force performance on his part.

In *Star Trek II*, all the action revolves around Kirk. Khan, an old enemy, is out to do him harm. Spock and McCoy, old friends, are out to get him back to where he really belongs . . . on the command bridge of the starship *Enterprise*. In the midst of all these occurrences, Kirk is confronted with his ex-lover, Carol Marcus, and their son, David.

In accepting the changes that have taken place in his life, Kirk discovers that what he had feared had changed has actually remained the same . . . his ability to command the *Enterprise*.

William Shatner, through a series of understated manner- isms, speech inflections and other dramatic devices that only a learned stage and film actor could convey as he does, convinces the audience that Kirk's problems are quite real. This acceptance assures that the audience will accept the film as equally real.

The actor uses his highly interesting face to its fullest advan- tage, carefully controlling his muscles to betray just the right amount of confidence, lack of confidence, fatigue and renewed strength.

No motion picture is the result of the labors of one individual. William Shatner's performance in *Star Trek II*, however, is the single most potent driving force visible to the audience.

Aided by the extremely capable performers Leonard Nimoy and DeForest Kelley, as well as the others of the cast, Shatner also makes the audience easy prey for sharing the agony over the loss of his friend, Mr. Spock.

The Kobayashi Maru test, which Kirk had previously cheated on to win, is again taken by him in this movie. Taking into account all that has happened to him during the unfolding of this latest *Star Trek* adventure, Kirk comes to terms with his loss, partially because he is now able to accept the presence of his son.

Due to Shatner's performance, the audience also takes (and passes) the same test of loss and acceptance of reality.

Shatner is truly a unique performer. Much of what *Star Trek* fans perceive as the reality of the *Trek* universe is actually an acceptance of the strength and reality that William Shatner transfuses into his alter ego, James T. Kirk.

DeForest Kelley

The 1967 World Science Fiction Convention was held in New York City. It was there that *Star Trek*'s second season of episodes had its debut when the segment "Amok Time" was screened. There are many good moments in this significant episode, but the moment that drew the most thunderous applause from the fans was the first viewing of the new screen credit ". . . and DeForest Kelley . . ." In Kelley's capable hands, the role of Dr. Leonard McCoy grew progressively more significant to the *Star Trek* format.

Kelley is a remarkable actor who brings sincerity and trust to the character of McCoy. He instills his role with a distinctive, fatherly attitude that makes the viewers instantly comfortable in his presence. At the same time, DeForest imbues McCoy with a timeless virility. These two qualities combine to make Bones an intriguing, believable and charismatic character.

Among *Star Trek* fans, there are those who like William Shatner more than Leonard Nimoy, and vice versa. Most all *Trek* fans, however, are in agreement that they like DeForest Kelley. When *Star Trek* ceased to be a television series in production and became a modern myth popular across the world, DeForest Kelley's popularity grew with the status of the show. He ceased forever to be a character actor and achieved that most elusive of distinctions: stardom.

QUESTION—*How does it feel to know you're a part of this contemporary mythology?*

DK — It's an unreal feeling, more or less, for me. I've never really accepted it as such. It keeps hitting me . . . and everytime something phenomenal happens, I think, *There it is again.* And you keep thinking that it's something that's going to go away. But it isn't going to go away, and it never will go away; it looks like it's really here to stay now, in one form or another. I try not to think about it too much, and I try desperately, as Harve Bennett and a few other people will tell you, to conduct my life as simply as possible. And in so doing, I'm sure I've altered my career a lot; a great deal of it has been my own fault. As I've very honestly said at conventions, and to other people, I've become extremely lazy in the last few years. Not altogether lazy, but disenchanted with a great deal of what I see on television and would really like to be a part of. There is so much on television that I look at and think, "Well, I've done that a long time ago. . . . If I had not become somewhat financially secure, I would be out there working my butt off at anything I could get. And *Star Trek* has done another thing, too. *Star Trek* wasn't like any other series that anyone has ever done. If you look in *The Star Trek Compendium,* you'll see that I've done a lot of westerns and what-have-you. Everything's in there over a great number of years. There are series that could become incredibly dull to do. Now, we didn't have a winner everytime out with *Star Trek,* but the one thing we did have was that there was always something interesting or challenging in each script, that kind of zipped you out and kept you going through it. And that's not too possible with a western or a detective series, with the exception of a very few. And when we came out of *Star Trek,* speaking for myself, I was somewhat spoiled, to a degree. Things that were offered to me were not appetizing at all as an actor. . . . There's been nothing to juice me up, that really made me want to go and do something. That's the best way to describe it. I don't know; I don't seem to worry about it, I'm not really unhappy with my situation as such. I'm really a very contented man, and I'm very pleased to be a part of *Star Trek* because I think it is a phenomenal thing to be associated with."

Q — *Do you have any negative feelings about the entire phenomenon at all?*

DK — I did for a while. Frankly, when I came out of *Star Trek,* I was offered a number of things, and I turned them down. They just did not appeal to me. I thought, well, for once in my life, I'm really in a position where I don't have to take it because I need it. If you look over my background, you will see that I have, in my own way and in my own time, done some good things. I've been associated with some awfully good people and I've experienced a lot of excitement, starting on this [Paramount] lot in 1946 as a young kid when they brought me up here to do *This Gun for Hire*; eventually, Alan Ladd did that. But you know, I was here at the tail end of the glamour period, when you couldn't walk down the street of this lot without having to duck around people, there was so much activity. Every sound stage was filled, and they had a loft where the dancers hoofed all day long, preparing for the musicals. It was a different picture altogether. The place across from the studio that's now a nursery was Lucy's; it was a famous restaurant where all the stars came from Metro and Fox. They had a big garden out there, and you could walk in at lunchtime and see every big star in Hollywood there.

Q — *Then in a sense, coming back to the studio for you is like it is to Sulu coming back to the* Enterprise *in the movie?*

DK — That's right. I've experienced a great deal of that in my lifetime, even to the popularity. I did a film here called *Fear in the Night,* my first film. It was a little film that became a sleeper, and it also became tremendously popular. . . . It was a completely new experience. And it was not unlike *Star Trek,* when the popularity started to explode; so I have that in the back of my life, too. I think, if I were talking to a psychiatrist, it would have a lot to do with my mental approach to the motion picture business today.

DeForest Kelley in an informal portrait

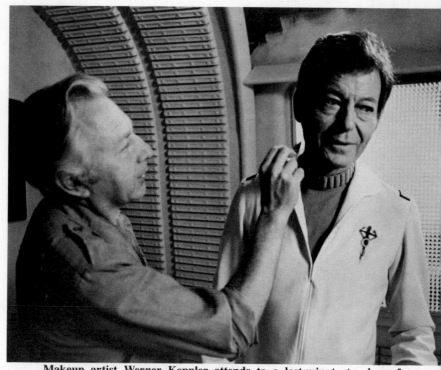

Makeup artist Werner Keppler attends to a last-minute touch-up for DeForest Kelley

Dr. McCoy recovers from his sudden death during the *Kobayashi Maru* test

Q — *Have you found that your life has either changed or become enriched by feedback emanating from the* Star Trek *fans with whom you come into contact?*

DK — Yes . . . by all means. There has been an enormous satisfaction. I think the *Star Trek* fans are unlike any other group of fans in the world. They're the most devoted group of people . . . encompassing all ages, and from all walks in life. This is certainly reflected in mail, which comes from doctors, lawyers, possibly the biggest university audience in the world, Mensa . . . from every walk of life. It's been an experience that I don't think many other actors have had an opportunity to have. It's instant recognition, wherever you go. But there's been a great deal of satisfaction, and to repeat a hackneyed statement, it's been a mixed blessing in that until *Star Trek* came along, I was a solid working actor, going from one job to another, enjoying it, playing a lot of heavies, having a lot of fun. There was a lot of excitement mixed in with it. None of us ever expected it to happen this way. I only knew that when I was doing the series, I knew we were doing something exceptional. Like I told Gene [Roddenberry], "You've either got the biggest hit or the biggest miss in the world." And it turned out to be both. It wasn't a hit with the ratings, but it is with the people. There are certain satisfactions; I'm able to do certain things as a result of *Star Trek* that I ordinarily would not be able to do. It's robbed me of privacy. I still try to keep it, and I've succeeded to a certain degree. I still live in an area that is best described as a *Saturday Evening Post* neighborhood, and I love it. I know the people there, they know me. If I'm out in front painting, or digging a rose garden, it's just, "Hi, De."

Q — *How do the neighborhood kids react toward you?*

DK — When new kids come into the neighborhood, invariably one of the kids who already lives there will bring them around to prove that I actually live there, that Dr. McCoy lives here. I

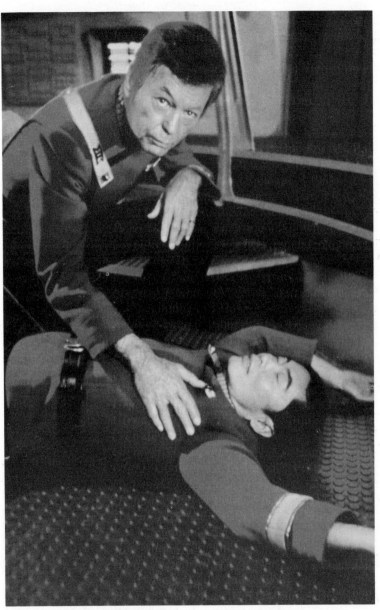

Sulu's death: the *Kobayashi Maru* episode

make it a point to meet them, and to get to know them, and once I get to talking to them and seeing them, they just pass me off like they do the mailman.

Q — *Is this situation the same since the release of* Star Trek II?

DK — . . . I don't know what this motion picture is going to do with [the privacy situation]. It's getting more hectic, since *Star Trek II* is such a big hit in the theaters. I've already noticed a tremendous difference.

Q — *Is there anything about your involvement with* Star Trek *that you're not happy about?*

DK — I don't have many complaints, but this is one thing that upset me in the past. In the first movie, Persis [Khambatta] replaced me in the newspaper ad copy. . . . And this time, of course, the same thing happened. It jarred me when I saw it.

Q — *How did you first become involved with* Star Trek? *You're so much a part of the series that it's strange to recall you didn't become involved until after the two pilots had been produced.*

DK — Gene Roddenberry screened the first pilot, which starred Jeffrey Hunter, for me. I had just finished a two-part *Bonanza* on this lot. He said he wanted me to look at it. I had done a pilot for Gene called *333 Montgomery,* in which I portrayed a lawyer. Gene had always been high on me as an actor, so I looked at this film *(The Cage)* and I saw John Hoyt as the ship's doctor, who had this one scene in the picture with Jeffrey Hunter (in which he functioned as the Captain's bartender and doctor all at once). And that was the role that he had in mind for me. I saw it and was fascinated by it. Something told me this role could really grow into a good thing, so I had a discussion with Gene, and I said, "Yes, I'd like very much to do it." I said if I work hard on it, and the people recognize this character, it can hopefully grow into something. Then it turned out that somebody, I didn't know who it was, didn't want me in the first place. When they recast it and got Bill Shatner, I wasn't in the pilot . . . they had turned me down.

Q — *The role of Dr. Mark Piper was played by Paul Fix, who had essayed much the same types of roles as you had in your career.*

DK — That's right.

Q — *But in "Where No Man Has Gone Before," the doctor had almost no direct interaction with the cast.*

DK — Some of that you have to create for yourself. We'd stop and discover things between Spock and myself . . . the relationship was more or less there in the beginning with Bill; it just developed with Leonard and myself. We enlarged upon it every chance we got. Whatever was put down, we tried to enlarge upon that, and sure enough he [McCoy] began to grow. Thanks to Gene Roddenberry, it had become quite a good role in the third year. If we had gone the fourth, we were discussing going on a rotating basis, featuring one character one week and one during another. But, of course, that year never came to pass.

The *Enterprise* Crew

". . . Just one big, happy fleet," commented Khan Noonian Singh sarcastically about Starfleet, and in the context of *Star Trek II: The Wrath of Khan* he was completely correct. Producing a motion picture is one of the most complex artistic feats in the entire world. It requires the talents of extraordinary people, working on both sides of the camera, who are sometimes called upon to accomplish the impossible.

In front of the cameras are the actors, those about whom the public is most aware. They begin each picture with nothing, and through their labors people come to life on film. If actors are lucky, they are given opportunities to create and recreate the same characterization so that the individual assimilates a bit of them, as well as taking on the characteristics of their creation. This may result in the performer being "typecast," but it also results in people becoming thoroughly acquainted with the character, to the extent that for anyone else to play the role would be unthinkable. This firmly established identity is a phenomenon of art.

In the classic science fiction movie *Forbidden Planet,* a scientist created a three-dimensional statue of his daughter, in miniature, using an advanced alien machine. When the spaceship commander observed the statuette moving, apparently alive, the scientist answered, "That's because my daughter is alive in my mind from micro-second to micro-second." Such is the case with the personnel of the starship *Enterprise*. Each has an established fan following. Each actor is extremely proficient at recalling his creation at a moment's notice (which is sometimes necessary during a film's production).

On the other side of the camera, and in fact permitting the camera to function, are people equally important but exposed much less to the public eye. It is only comparatively recently that motion picture fans have started to take note of the contributions of these behind-the-scenes artists. Beginning with the producer, who plans the entire film, progressing to the writers who devise the script and arriving at the designers and cinematographers who transfer the script onto film with the aid of the performers, each individual involved in this process is a necessary and vital part of the miraculous process that culminates in the completion of a motion picture.

Every person involved does his best; as Mr. Spock would observe, "Each according to his gifts."

The Actors

James Doohan (Scotty)

In *Star Trek II,* Montgomery Scott confesses to having suffered through ". . . a wee bout of shore leave," coped with by using Dr. McCoy's 23rd Century medicine. In reality, actor James Doohan recently recovered from something far more serious—a heart attack. Fortunately, Mr. Doohan is a rare individual, filled with vital energy and liked and respected by hundreds of thousands of fans all over the world. If it were possible for Jimmy's many fans to transfer their strength into him, they would have done so without a moment's hesitation. Considering the high regard for the man, it's possible that may account for at least a part of the reason for Doohan's wonderful recovery.

The dynamism of Montgomery Scott matches that of his interpreter, Mr. Doohan. One of the most memorable moments in *Star Trek II* is the entrance of Scotty onto the *Enterprise* bridge carrying the body of a young, unidentified crewman. The original script called for the young man to be identified as Scotty's

Enterprise **Chief Engineer Montgomery Scott (James Doohan)**

nephew; these lines, however, were ultimately edited out of the movie. It seems more appropriate the way it remains in the finished film, because Scotty would grieve over any *Enterprise* crewman who was injured in the line of duty, especially if they were hurt while protecting his beloved engines, as young Mr. Preston was.

Walter Koenig (Mr. Chekov)

With his knowledge of *Star Trek*, his exposure to the behind-the-scenes occurrences and his knowledge of psychology, Walter Koenig could write a wonderful book about *Star Trek*. In fact, he already has: Pocket Book's *Chekov's Enterprise*, a chronicle of what transpired during the production of *Star Trek: The Motion Picture*. Walter is a delight to talk with at conventions. He is very unlike the average celebrity, occasionally taking walks through dealers' areas and often stopping to chat with fans who are delighted that one of the *Trek* stars would take the time to communicate directly with them.

Walter Koenig is a multifaceted individual. Besides his skill at acting he has also taught acting and written scripts.

Walter Koenig: Commander Chekov

In *Star Trek II,* Pavel Chekov is also a multifaceted character, dominated by Khan and the Ceti Eels. For his role, Walter endured many unhappy hours sitting completely still while synthetic eels were guided over his face. He also suffered while wearing the extremely uncomfortable spacesuits in the opening of the Ceti Alpha V sequence. Lastly, Chekov did a lot of screaming before recovering from the effects of the eels.

The next time you see *Star Trek II,* note that Chekov is not completely recovered when he makes his entrance onto the bridge. Actor Koenig added mannerisms to his entrance that suggested there was some (temporary?) trauma suffered by Chekov.

George Takei (Sulu)

Outgoing George Takei's presence is eagerly anticipated by *Star Trek* fans due to the actor's very friendly personality and his enthusiasm for making new friends and discussing his work with fans. George is well known for his wonderfully unabandoned laugh and his equally open sense of humor.

George Takei has recently acted on television in segments of *Vegas* and *Magnum P.I.* and has appeared as the host/narrator of a PBS special on cryogenics entitled *Life Can Be Frozen.*

Besides his acting career, George is actively involved in politics. In 1972, he was an official delegate to the Miami Beach Democratic Presidential Convention. The following year he was a candidate for the Los Angeles City Council seat vacated by Mayor Bradley. In 1974 he was a delegate to the Mid-Term Conference in Kansas City, and two years later George became an alternate to the New York Presidential Convention (resulting in his being invited to the Washington inaugural festivities).

George was also appointed to the Board of Directors of the Southern California Rapid Transit District, representing the city of Los Angeles. He is also a vice-president of the American Public Transportation Association.

In *Star Trek II,* it is George's character of Sulu who guides Admiral Kirk back to the *Enterprise* and observes that he is always grateful for the nostalgic experience of visiting their old ship. *Star Trek* fans, of course, agree with this observation, and

George Takei: Mr. Sulu

are also aware that a trip on board the starship *Enterprise* would not be quite the same without the hand of Sulu guiding the giant vessel through space.

Nichelle Nichols (Uhura)

Nichelle Nichols, actress and singer, is one of those rare people who prove that mortals need not be afraid of the effects of time. She is virtually ageless, extremely feminine and generally a

Nichelle Nichols: Communications Chief Uhura

pleasure to speak with at conventions. Between her organization, Women In Motion, and her affiliations with NASA's minority astronaut recruitment program, she is an unusually capable human being whose *Star Trek* career has endeared her to countless fans of many countries.

Bibi Besch: Dr. Carol Marcus

Bibi Besch (Dr. Carol Marcus)

Bibi Besch, the daughter of famed stage actress Gusti Huber, is a welcome addition to the *Star Trek* motion picture family. The attractive artist contributes yet another vital screen presence to the *Trek* universe.

Ms. Besch, whose interests include a specialized form of yoga, is an excellent cook; undoubtedly her line in *Star Trek II,* "Can I cook?" regarding Dr. Marcus's Genesis invention, is sheer coincidence.

We hope we will be seeing more of Dr. Marcus in future *Star Trek* feature films. We also look forward to seeing Bibi Besch at *Star Trek* conventions. She promises to be a most delightful guest, as evidenced by her outgoing appearances on talk shows and her statement that she would like to attend *Star Trek* conventions.

Ms. Besch, whose career has included a variety of motion picture and television appearances, lives with her young daughter, whom she describes as her best friend.

Bibi Besch's Credits

STAGE

Cherry Orchard, The
Chinese Prime Minister, The (Broadway)
Evening of Frost Poetry, An
Fame (Broadway)
Here Lies Jeremy Troy (Broadway)
Macbeth

FILMS

Beast Within, The
Hardcore
Meteor
New York Experience, The (Trans-Lux, 1973, narration)
Promise, The (with Stephen Collins)

TELEVISION

Backstairs at the White House (NBC miniseries, 1979)
Death of a Centerfold (Television Movie)
Hart to Hart (title and year unknown)
Kate Columbo (title and year unknown)
Love Is a Many Splendored Thing (CBS soap opera; appeared regularly as Iris Garrison, 1972–73)
Peter Lundy and the Medicine Hat Stallion (NBC Television Movie, 1977)
Police Woman (title and year unknown)
Rockford Files, The (title and year unknown)

Secrets of Midland Heights (CBS series, recurring role as Dorothy Wheeler, 1980–81)

Secret Storm, The (CBS soap opera, recurring role for two years)

Somerset (NBC soap opera, appeared regularly for 3 years as Eve Lawrence)

Steeltown (CBS Television Movie, 1979)

Three Times Daley (CBS series pilot, 1976)

Tom and Joann (CBS series pilot, 1978)

Transplant (Television Movie)

Victory at Entebbe (Television Movie)

Merritt Butrick (Dr. David Marcus)

Merritt Butrick, who brings the character of Dr. David Marcus to life, was born September 3, 1959, in Gainesville, Florida. Raised in the San Francisco, California, area, he earned a B.A. degree in fine arts from the California Institute of the Arts in Valencia, California.

Merritt has appeared in a total of 22 Northern California regional theater productions, as well as in the motion picture *The Wiz Kid*.

On television, he has guest-starred in episodes of *Chips, Hill Street Blues* and CBS' *Square Pegs*.

Bearing a striking facial resemblence to William Shatner, which was necessary for his being able to play the role of Admiral James Kirk's son, Merritt conveys subtle strength to audiences watching *Star Trek II: The Wrath of Khan*. Quiet, stubborn, filled with intelligence and a concern that the ways of peace will prevail throughout the Federation planets, the character of David is very much like what Kirk must have been like in his days at Starfleet Academy.

Paul Winfield: Captain Clark Terrell

Paul Winfield (Captain Terrell)

Paul Winfield, the magnetic performer who portrays Captain Clark Terrell, was born in Los Angeles in 1940. He first developed an interest in the performing arts when he appeared in the Edison Junior High School senior play.

Paul attended Manual Arts High School in Los Angeles and became the first student there to win the school's best actor award three times in a row in their annual drama competition. He began acting while at the school in 1962.

The recipient of several college scholarships, Winfield attended U.C.L.A. and graduated with a B.A. degree in theater.

Paul's first big break in acting was courtesy of Burgess Meredith, who cast him in two one-act plays written by LeRoi Jones. His initial parts were mostly in stage productions, followed by his first television and motion picture assignments.

Winfield was associated with the Stanford University repertory company and with the Inner City Cultural Theatre in Los Angeles.

The actor won wide acclaim for his portrayal of the Rev. Dr. Martin Luther King in the television feature "King," a demanding role in which he ably recreated this complex and remarkable man.

In his role as Terrell in *Star Trek II*, Winfield is not involved in the bulk of the film's action, but he nevertheless injects a great deal of life into his role, making audiences feel that he appears in more of the film than he actually does. His character's death scene is extremely effective and makes the viewers of the movie wish that Terrell did not have to leave the *Star Trek* universe just after we were introduced to him.

Paul Winfield's Credits

STAGE

Dutchman
Toilet, The

MOTION PICTURES

Brother John (Columbia, 1971)
Conrack (20th Century-Fox, 1974)
Damnation Alley (20th Century-Fox, 1977)
Gordon's War (20th Century-Fox, 1973)
Greatest, The (Columbia, 1977)
Hero Ain't Nothin' but a Sandwich, A (New World, 1977)
High Velocity (Turtle/First Asian Films, 1976)
Huckleberry Finn (United Artists, 1974)
Hustle (Paramount, 1975)

Paul Winfield and Walter Koenig between takes

R.P.M. (Columbia, 1970)
Sounder (20th Century-Fox, Academy Award Nomination: Best
    Actor)
Trouble Man (20th Century-Fox, 1972)
Twilight's Last Gleaming (Allied Artists, 1977)
White Dog (1982)

TELEVISION

Backstairs at the White House (NBC miniseries: Emmett Rogers,
    Sr., 1979, with Bibi Besch)
Cowboy in Africa (title unknown, 1967)
Green Eyes (data unknown)
High Chaparral (title unknown, 1969)
Horror at 37,000 Feet, The (CBS Television Movie, 1973, with
    William Shatner)
Ironside ("Find a Victim," 1972)
    ("Robert Phillips Vs. the Man," 1968)

It's Good to Be Alive (CBS special, 1974)
James Garner Show, The ("Eddie Joe," 1972)
Julia ("It takes Two to Tangle," 1969; recurring role as Paul
  Carter, Julia's boyfriend)
  (title unknown, 1969)
  (title unknown, 1970)
King (NBC Television Movie, 1978; Emmy nomination for Best
  Actor)
King of the Line (Television Movie, year unknown)
Mannix ("The Odds Against Donald," 1969)
Mission: Impossible ("Trial by Fury," 1968)
Name of the Game, The ("The Suntan Mob," 1969)
Room 222 (title unknown, 1969)
Roots: The Next Generations (ABC television miniseries, 1979)
Sophistocated Gents (data unknown)
Young Lawyers, The ("A Simple Thing Called Justice," 1970)
Young Rebels, The ("Unbroken Chains," 1970)

Kirstie Alley (Saavik)

Actress Kirstie Alley knew her way around the starship
Enterprise years before she first set foot on the Paramount studio
lot. Like many of us, Kirstie grew up watching *Star Trek,* wishing
that she could be a part of the optimistic explorations of the
spaceship. She was particularly intrigued with the character of
Mr. Spock and spent a great deal of time practicing "Vulcan"
walks and facial expressions. These researches eventually led to
her getting the role of Saavik; director Nicholas Meyer had
interviewed many other actresses for this role and had almost
made up his mind about another young performer when Ms. Alley
entered the picture.

Kirstie's sense of humor was praised by everyone who
worked with her. Between takes, she and Merritt Butrick would
dance around the sets, brightening up the atmosphere, helping to
ease the tension of deadlines.

Ms. Alley, who was born and raised in Wichita, Kansas,
made her motion picture acting debut in *Star Trek II*. She turned

Lt. Saavik at her station (Kirstie Alley)

in a marvelous performance, allowing just the right amount of her sense of humor to show in the character of Saavik.

The half-Vulcan, half-Romulan Lt. Saavik is one of the most interesting characters in the *Star Trek* universe. Hopefully, in the next *Star Trek* feature, we will learn more about her. Perhaps a relationship will develop between her and David Marcus. Such a relationship was originally scheduled to occur in *Star Trek II,* but due to the large amount of interplay that was already visible on screen the scenes were cut.

The Men Behind the Scenes

Star Trek II was fortunate to have a staff of technical artists who were just right for the job of translating this difficult project to the screen.

Writer Jack B. Sowards, a science fiction fan, was the individual who Harve Bennett credits with first getting the idea to kill Mr. Spock.

Director of Photography Gayne Rescher, like producer Robert Sallin, gained much of his experience in the high-pressure field of advertising, photographing commercials with impossible technical requirements and deadlines and doing it successfully.

Production Designer Joseph R. Jennings first worked on Warner Brothers films, then on the television series *Gunsmoke*. A friend of original starship *Enterprise* co-designer Matt Jefferies, Jennings also drew some of the series' designs, based upon Jefferies's plans. A co-designer of the new version of the *U.S.S. Enterprise,* Jennings is an extremely warm and honest human being, a delight to talk to and a gold mine of perceptions about the motion picture industry.

Editor William P. Dornisch also gained his experience in commercials.

Costume Designer Robert Fletcher brought the vibrant and diversified wardrobe of *Star Trek II* into existence.

Additional personnel include Associate Producer William F. Phillips, Unit Production Manager Austin Jewell, First Assistant Director Douglas E. Wise (another veteran of *Star Trek: The Motion Picture*), Art Director Michael Minor (who worked on the first *Trek* feature and whose work was also seen in the original TV episodes) and composer James Horner.

The Music of
Star Trek II

The success of any motion picture is directly based upon how believable it is to the moviegoer. There would be no purpose in watching a film without caring about the characters and what happens to them during the course of the adventure. A good script is the core of a good movie. There are other essentials as well: good direction, photography and design. One of the most important requirements is the presence of a good musical score. Music aids the audience in experiencing whatever reactions the filmmakers are attempting to instill with them. The score to *Star Trek II: The Wrath of Khan* is completely successful in doing what it sets out to accomplish. This is due to the talent of the score's composer, James Horner.

Horner, whose previous credits include numerous dramatic films, gives no hint from his work that his age is 28. He has full command of the orchestra; he knows what he is doing, and he does it exceedingly well.

Director Nicholas Meyer wanted the score to have the same qualities as an adventure film set on the high seas. Although Starfleet is a military organization, and the *Enterprise* is certainly the futuristic equivalent of a warship (a "ship of the line," as Admiral Hornblower would call it), his prime concern was that the audience feel the thrill of adventurous travel. This is a distinct switch from recent science fiction films, which accentuate military pomp in their scores.

Horner learned of the choice assignment from Joel Sill, vice-president of music for the motion picture division of Paramount Pictures. He was introduced to Harve Bennett, Robert Sallin and Nicholas Meyer. Meyer, who has a strong interest in film music, helped to determine specifically what sort of score was needed in the movie.

James began to compose the score toward the middle of January, 1982. He had five weeks to complete his demanding task. During that time, he created approximately seventy minutes of music, half of which appear on the Atlantic Records soundtrack album for the movie.

During the five weeks of composition, he assured the success of the film's last three reels of decisive action.

The scoring sessions lasted for five days, making use of a ninety-piece symphony orchestra managed by Carl Fortina. Horner himself conducted his score. Orchestrations were written by Jack Hayes, and in the finished film the music was edited by Robert Badami.

The soundtrack album for the film contains 44 minutes, 35 seconds worth of music, which include renditions of the opening portion of Alexander Courage's original *Star Trek* series theme.

In the composer's opinion, a little less music should have been included in the album, due to limitations in today's recording procedures. The composer's worry regarding the recorded score was that the music recorded in the grooves closest to the center of the disc would be too constricted to reproduce the fullest range of the melodies' sound.

One of the most rewarding experiences that can occur to a composer of motion picture program music is being told that his music makes a sequence work in the best manner possible. In *Star Trek II*, there was some doubt about whether or not the short sequence on the surface of the newly formed Genesis Planet would be used in the final print. This doubt apparently persisted until the score was recorded. At the recording session, the composer remembers, the emotional impact of his music, juxtaposed with the scene taken in context with the rest of the workprint, led at least one of the film's production people to weep from the sheer beauty of the sequence.

Mr. Horner listened to none of the tapes of the music written for the original *Star Trek* television series. Instead, he went by Meyer's suggestions and his own perceptions to produce the score.

One of the most interesting pieces is Mr. Spock's theme. Only 1 minute, 10 seconds in length, the mood created by this piece of music completely describes the sensitivity, conflict and loneliness of the character we have all come to know. The composer's original intention when writing this piece was to locate an electronic instrument called an Ondes Martinot, which produces a distinctive, plaintive tone. Unfortunately, no one could locate this rare French instrument anywhere in this country, and Horner instead settled for recreating the sound of the instrument as closely as possible.

For the scenes describing the insane characer of Khan Noonian Singh, the intent was the opposite from that regarding Spock's music. Confusion, frustration and a pronounced crazed quality are present in the score in such a way that the audience is not distracted by any overstated "madness" theme. Still, we know something is terribly wrong with this man as we hear purposely inserted discordant sounds in the background of the themes describing the man.

For the band entitled "Khan's Pets," which ran a little over four minutes in its finished state, we *hear* the repugnant, slimy qualities of the "Wee Beasties."

Horner felt that the opening portion of Alexander Courage's TV series theme should be retained in his score. This questing melody, which suggests the essence of exploration that drives Kirk to journey on mission after mission, is called "Where no man has gone before." Its presence in the film's opening credits is a musical statement of executive producer Harve Bennett's intention to preserve and present as many points about the original *Star Trek* format as possible.

In addition to the presence of Courage's theme, Horner's music is exciting and free. It plainly suggests a tall ship sailing to parts unknown and is similar in spirit to composer Bronislau Kaper's opening title theme in the remake of MGM's *Mutiny on the Bounty*.

In contrast to this theme of vastness and expansion is the claustrophobic and uncertain flavor present in the "Mutara Nebula" theme. This portion of the film was intended by Bennett and Meyer to resemble a World War II submarine warfare situation in which each ship is equally matched against the other due to a lack of working sensor equipment and extreme weather conditions. Horner's music carries this illusion across to the audience.

The film's epilogue and end credits are filled with hope, indicating that Kirk's career has been resumed, the *Enterprise* sails on and that *Star Trek* will be returning in subsequent adventures. When it does, let's hope that composer James Horner will compose the score that helps to describe the adventures of the *Enterprise* and its crew.

Cast and Credits
Star Trek II:
The Wrath of Khan

CAST

Kirk . . . . WILLIAM SHATNER
Spock . . . . LEONARD NIMOY
McCoy . . . . DEFOREST KELLEY
Scotty . . . . JAMES DOOHAN
Chekov . . . . WALTER KOENIG
Sulu . . . . GEORGE TAKEI
Uhura . . . . NICHELLE NICHOLS
Carol . . . . BIBI BESCH
David . . . . MERRITT BUTRICK
Terrell . . . . PAUL WINFIELD
Saavik . . . . KIRSTIE ALLEY
Khan . . . . RICARDO MONTALBAN
Preston . . . . IKE EISENMANN
Jedda . . . . JOHN VARGAS
Kyle . . . . JOHN WINSTON
Beach . . . . PAUL KENT
Cadet . . . . NICHOLAS GUEST
Madison . . . . RUSSELL TAKAKI
March . . . . KEVIN SULLIVAN
Crew Chief . . . . JOEL MARSTAN
Bridge Voice . . . . TERESA E. VICTOR
Radio Voices . . . . DIANNE HARPER, DAVID RUPRECHT
Computer Voice . . . . MARCY VOSBURGH
Stunts . . . . STEVE BLALOCK, JANET BRADY, JIM BURK,
        DIANE CARTER, TONY CECERE, ANN CHATTERTON, GARY COMBS, GILBERT
        COMBS, JIM CONNORS, BILL COUCH, SR., BILL COUCH, JR., EDDY DONNO,
    JOHN ESKOBAR, ALLAN GRAF, CHUCK HICKS, TOMMY J. HUFF, HUBIE KERNS,
        JR., PAULA MOODY, TOM MORGA, BETH NUFFER, MARY PETERS,
            ERNEST ROBINSON, JOHN ROBOTHAM, KIM WASHINGTON,
                MIKE WASHLAKE, GEORGE WILBUR

CREDITS

Directed by ....Nicholas Meyer
Produced by ....Robert Sallin
Screenplay by ....Jack B. Sowards
Story by ....Harve Bennett, Jack B. Sowards
Executive Producer ....Harve Bennett
Based on *Star Trek*, Created by ....Gene Roddenberry
Director of Photography ....Gayne Rescher, A.S.C.
Production Designer ....Joseph R. Jennings
Edited by ....William P. Dornisch
Music Composed by ....James Horner
Executive Consultant ....Gene Roddenberry
Associate Producer ....William F. Phillips
Costume Designer ....Robert Fletcher
Unit Production Manager ....Austen Jewell
First Assistant Director ....Douglas E. Wise
Second Assistant Director ....Richard Espinoza
Art Director ....Michael Minor
Set Decorator ....Charles M. Graffeo
Camera Operator ....Craig Denault
First Camera Assistant ....Catherine Coulson
Second Camera Assistant ....Tom Connole
Sound Mixer ....Jim Alexander
Boom ....Patrick Clark
Recordist ....Mark S. Server
Wardrobe Supervisors ....James Linn, Agnes G. Henry
Wardrobe ....Kimon Beazlie, Joseph Markham, Robin Michel Bush
Makeup Artists ....Werner Keppler, James L. McCoy
Hair Stylist ....Dione Taylor
Script Supervisor ....Mary Jane Ferguson
Special Effects Supervisor ....Bob Dawson
Special Effects . .Edward A. Ayer, Martin Becker, Gary F. Bentley, Fred
        Brauer, Peter G. Evangelatos, William Purcell, Harry Stewart
Additional Special Lighting Effects ....Sam Nicholson
Gaffer ....Romolo Acquistapace
Best Boy ....Charles Langham
Best Boy ....Murphy Wiltz
Key Grip ....Gene Griffith
Second Grip ....Tom James
Dolly Grip ....Don Whipple
Crane Operator ....Gary L. Jensen
Property Master ....Joe Longo
Assistant Property Master ....Charles C. Equia
Lead Man ....Michael Friedman
Swing Gang ....Michael C. Gian, John Graffeo
Construction Coordinator ....Al DeGaetano
Carpenters ......C.R. Bulys, Edward Charnock, Jr., David D. Gabrielli,
                Jerry Luthart, Clinton Madkins, Milius Romyn
Standby Painter ....Ric Paronelli
Set Designers ....Daniel Gluck, Daniel E. Maltese

Graphic Designer .... Lee Cole
Video Coordinator .... Todd Grodnick
Transportation Coordinator .... Mike McDuffee
Transportation Captain .... Rick Valencia
Transportation Co-Captain .... Howard Davidson
Drivers ... Patrick Connor, Tim Roslan, Rick Sanders, Murray Schwartz
Stunt Coordinator .... Bill Couch
Craft Service .... Terry Ahern
DGA Trainee .... Sandra M. Middleton
Set Security .... Jeff Melichar
Auditor .... Stephen Brener
Unit Publicist .... Edward Egan
Still Photographer .... Bruce Birmelin
Post-Production Coordinator .... Ralph Winter
Assistant Editors ... John A. Haggar, Christopher L. Koefoed, Vicky Witt
Supervising Sound Editors .... Cecilia Hall, George Watters II
Sound Effects Editors .. Teresa Eckton, Michael Hilkene, John Kline, Jim
Siracusa, Curt Schulkey
Assistant Sound Effects Editors .... John Colwell, Dan Finnerty
Foley Editor .... Tony Palk
Special Sound Effects .... Alan Howarth
Additional Sound Effects .... Eugene Finley
Loop Editors .... Jack Keath, Cliff Bell, Jr.
Music Editor .... Robert Badami
Orchestrations .... Jack Hayes
Scoring Mixer .... Dan Wallin, Record Plant Scoring
Re-Recording Mixers ... Ray West, C.A.S., David J. Hudson, Mel Metcalfe
Dolby Stereo Consultant .... David W. Gray
Color Timer .... Bob Nolan
Negative Cutter .... Dode Weyant
Casting .... Mary V. Buck
Casting Assistant .... Kim Diane Fleary
Assistant to Harve Bennett .... Sylvia Rubinstein
Assistant to Gene Roddenberry .... Susan Sackett
Secretary to Nicholas Meyer .... Janna R. Wong
Production Office Secretary .... Lea Andrews
Technical Advisor .... Dr. Richard Green
Title Design .... Don Kracke, Rodger Johnson
Vulcan Translation .... Marc Okrand
Assistant to the Producers .... Deborah Arakelian

Special Visual Effects
Produced at
Industrial Light & Magic
A Division of Lucasfilm, Ltd.
Marin County, California

Special Visual Effects Supervisors .... Jim Veilleux
Ken Ralston
Effects Cameramen .... Don Dow
Scott Farrar

Camera Operator .... Stewart Barbee

Assistant Camera Operators. .SELWYN EDDY III, DAVID HARDBERGER, ROBERT HILL, MIKE OWENS, MICHAEL SANTY
Optical Photography Supervisor . . . . .BRUCE NICHOLSON
Optical Printer Operators. . . . . .DAVID BERRY, KENNETH SMITH, MARK VARGO, JOHN ELLIS, DONALD CLARK
Optical Line-up . . . . .THOMAS ROSSETER, ED JONES, RALPH GORDON
Optical Laboratory Technicians . . . . .TIM GEIDEMAN, DUNCAN MYERS, BOB CHRISOULIS
General Manager, ILM . . . . .TOM SMITH
Production Supervisor . . . . .PATRICIA ROSE DUIGNAN
Production Coordinator. . . . . .WARREN FRANKLIN
Matte Painting Artists . . . . .CHRIS EVANS, FRANK ORDAZ
Matte Photography . . . . .NEIL KREPELA
Matte Photography Assistant . . . . .CRAIG BARRON
Supervising Modelmaker . . . . .STEVE GAWLEY
Modelmakers . . . . . . .WILLIAM GEORGE, SEAN CASEY, LARRY TAN, JEFF MANN, STEVE SANDERS, BRIAN CHIN, BOB DIEPENBROCK, MIKE FULMER
Model Electronics. . . . . .MARTY BRENNEIS
Animation Supervisor. . . . . .SAMUEL COMSTOCK
Animators . .KIM KNOWLTON, SCOTT CAPLE, JIM KEEFER, KATHRYN LENIHAN, JUDY ELKINS, JAY DAVIS
Additional Animation . . . . .VISUAL CONCEPT ENGINEERING
Supervising Effects Editor . . . . .ARTHUR REPOLA
Effects Editor. . . . . .PETER AMUNDSON
Computer Database Management. . . . . .MALCOLM BLANCHARD
Computer Graphics . .LOREN CARPENTER, ED CATMULL, PAT COLE, ROB COOK, TOM DUFF, ROBERT D. POOR, THOMAS PORTER, WILLIAM REEVES, ALVY RAY SMITH

Starfield Effects by	BRENT WATSON	*Tactical Displays by*
EVANS & SUTHERLAND	STEVE MCALLISTER	EVANS & SUTHERLAND
DIGISTAR SYSTEM	NEIL HARRINGTON	PICTURE SYSTEM
	JERI PANEK	

Molecular Computer Graphics by
COMPUTER GRAPHICS LABORATORY
UNIVERSITY OF CALIFORNIA
SAN FRANCISCO
DR. ROBERT LANGRIDGE

Still Photographer . . . . .TERRY CHOSTNER
Still Lab Technicians . . . . .ROBERTO MCGRATH, KERRY NORDQUIST
Supervising Stage Technician . . . . .T.E. MOEHNKE
Stage Technicians. . . . . .DAVE CHILDERS, HAROLD COLE, DICK DOVA, BOBBY FINLEY III, PATRICK FITZSIMMONS, EDWARD HIRSH, JOHN MCCLEOD, PETER STOLZ
Pyrotechnics. . . . . .THAINE MORRIS
Equipment Coordinator. . . . . .WADE CHILDRESS
Ultra High Speed Camera . . . . .BRUCE HILL PRODUCTIONS
Assistant to Tom Smith . . . . .KYLE TURNER
Travel Arrangements . . . . .KATHY SHINE

Grateful acknowledgment is made to the National Aeronautics and Space Administration and the Jet Propulsion Laboratory

Video Displays by THE BURBANK STUDIOS

Video Supervisor . . . . .HAL LANDAKER
Chief Engineer. . . . . .ALAN LANDAKER
Video Operators . . . . .MARVIN HOAR
ED MOSKOWITZ
JIM PADGETT

Additional Computer Graphics Furnished by Los Alamos National Laboratory
Additional Optical Effects by Modern Film Effects
Theme from *Star Trek* Television Series
Music by Alexander Courage
The Producers Acknowledge the Invaluable Assistance of Bjo Trimble,
Sonni Cooper, David Gerrold, Theodore Sturgeon and Samuel A.
Peeples in All Matters Relating to *Star Trek*

Filmed in Panavision®
Sound by Glen Glenn
Dolby® Stereo
Color by Movielab

Notes

THE DEATH OF MR. SPOCK

1. The *Wall Street Journal,* 9 October 1981. "Does Mr. Spock Die in the Next Episode of *Star Trek* Saga?" by Stephen J. Sansweet.
2. Dr. McCoy's return from the dead in "Shore Leave" (script by Theodore Sturgeon) suggests that "Bones" may now actually be a sophisticated android constructed in the planet's underground facilities. Scotty's resurrection in "The Changeling" is ironic in that the engineer, who can fix any machine, is himself restored to life by a machine.
3. The film's box office grosses are excellent. The home video version has yet to be released.
4. The *New York Post,* 25 November 1981. "Screen Scoops" (Trekkies United to Save Spock in New Enterprise), by Eric Kasum.
5. *Cinefantastique,* July/August, 1982, p. 73. *"Star Trek II,"* by Kay Anderson.
6. There was also a fourth possibility: that *Star Trek III* would take place *before* the story told in *Star Trek II.*
7. *Newsday,* 11 May 1982. "In Short" (Spock Dies in New Film).
8. The color values in the nebula sequence, among other things, had not yet been balanced.
9. More about this sequence in Chapters 15 and 17.

THE EARLIEST DRAFTS

1. This date, mentioned in this draft, is taken directly from the script for "Space Seed."
2. Khan and his followers actually succeeded in their aim for a brief while.
3. In later drafts, this dramatic occurrence took place close to the film's finish.
4. Here we have an example of a slight breach in Trek continuity: the series' male Vulcans all had names beginning with S.
5. The later drafts of the *Star Trek II* script would have no references to *Star Trek—The Motion Picture* at all.
6. Many elements of the final script are present, in some form, in the earlier drafts. This may have been the origin of the Genesis Cave.
7. Here, it appears as if Khan was studying with the Talosians of "The Cage," or the Melkots of "Spectre of the Gun."
8. Kirk obviously remembered Spock's emergency Vulcan mind-meld, which saved the lives of Kirk and company in "Spectre of the Gun" by convincing them " . . . The bullets are *not* real."

9. Dr. Janet Wallace was seen in the television episode "The Deadly Years"; she was an old friend of Kirk's, as well as one of the Federation's highest-rated endocrinologists.

10. On the television series, it was established that Kirk's having known someone in The Academy was tantamount to a death sentence.

11. Once again, a tribute to the scene in "Spectre of the Gun" wherein the bullets of the "Earps" pass harmlessly "through" our friends.

12. It is not explained how the *Enterprise,* in close proximity to an explosion of this magnitude, was not likewise destroyed.

13. One can only imagine how the Klingons and Romulans would react to news of this nature.

NICHOLAS MEYER

1. 1946 was also the year in which author H. G. Wells died.

2. *Target Practice,* published in 1974 by Harcourt Brace Jovanovich.

3. *The West End Horror: A Posthumous Memoir of John H. Watson, M.D., as edited by Nicholas Meyer,* published in 1976 by Dutton.

4. *Black Orchid,* by Nicholas Meyer and Barry Jay Kaplan, published in New York by Dial Press, 1977.

5. *Confessions of a Homing Pigeon,* published in 1981, Dial Press.

6. "Jack The Ripper Meets H. G. Wells On Film," *The New York Times,* 23 September, 1979, Sec. 2, p. 1, by Dan Yakir.

7. Ibid.

8. *Time After Time* was released in 1979 by Warner Brothers.

9. The screenplay for *Time After Time* was written by Nicholas Meyer, from a story by Karl Alexander Tunberg and Steven Hayes.

10. This film's shooting title was *The Honey Factor.* The screenplay, written by Nicholas Meyer, was dated January 15, 1973.

11. *The Seven Percent Solution* was released in 1976 by Universal Pictures.

Bibliography

Actors' Television Credits (1950–72)
by James Robert Parish
The Scarecrow Press, Inc., Metuchen, N.J., 1973.
(editing associates: Paige Lucas, Florence Solomon, T. Allan Taylor)

Actors' Television Credits (Supplement I)
by James Robert Parish, with Mark Trost
The Scarecrow Press, Inc., Metuchen, N.J. & London, 1978.

The Complete Directory to Prime Time Network TV Shows (1946–Present)
by Tim Brooks and Earle Marsh
Ballantine Books, New York, N.Y., 1979.

The Complete Encyclopedia of Television Programs (1947–76) (2 volumes)
by Vincent Terrace
A. S. Barnes & Co., Inc., Cranbury, N.J., 1976.

Forty Years of Screen Credits (1929–1969) (2 volumes)
compiled by John T. Weaver
The Scarecrow Press, Inc., Metuchen, N.J., 1970.

Television Drama Series Programming: A Comprehensive Chronicle, 1959–1975
by Larry James Gianakos
The Scarecrow Press, Inc., Metuchen, N.J. & London, 1978.